Beyond The Red Barn

Ted Lyons

BookLocker
Saint Petersburg, Florida

Dedicated to Carl Sagan, a dreamer....

"My own suspicion is that the universe is not
only queerer than we suppose,
but queerer than we can suppose."

J.B.S. Haldane

Prologue

**

You're in a bookstore. Remember bookstores? You see a book title or cover that intrigues you. But now, particularly if the author's unknown to you, you may have to slog through his/her interminable life story before you get to the reason for your investment. Comedian Steven Wright says when he wants to read someone's autobiography, he just skips to the about the author section on the back flap. He's a slightly off-center individual.

An interesting read is the George Martin book "All You Need Is Ears." I scanned the first third until I got to the meat of it, The Beatles. Before getting into the post Beatles third of the book I went back and reread the earlier parts I'd flipped through. It gave me some perspective and understanding of the famed producer and delivered some insight on the whys and wherefores of his Beatles recording decisions and interactions. It explained how a staid Englishman got caught up in the craziness of Beatlemania while helping to create the unorthodox recording techniques that came out of the Abbey Road studios.

George's well-worn book now resides in a favored position in my reading room, adjacent to the bathtub. If you want to take the time, an early chapter can sometimes answer unasked questions.

I've got this problem. I'm grateful for it and hope we all have it. I've always been acutely aware, even as a child, of the interconnectedness of life, of the "us." We're the pebble thrown into a pond creating ripples in all directions, affecting him or her, this or that, in ways of which we'll probably never become aware.

About five years ago I drove a couple to the airport. They seemed vaguely familiar. We were chatting, one road led to another and the big reveal was that I'd introduced them at a gig in 1976. It was break time. I was sitting with a guy whom I casually knew and called his future wife over under the pretense of helping me write out the next set. My subtle hit was to no avail as they danced the night away, left together, started dating, got married and forty years later wound up in the back seat of my Limo for a ride to Newark Airport. Ripples.

In my college dorm room, I had a Day-Glo poster of the infamous Acid Cat. It was just a large orange cat in a seated position observing the observer. Upon closer inspection the cat becomes a large map with trails and offshoots, dead ends and roads to nowhere. It was meant to be enjoyed in an elevated "frame of mind." Occasionally I'd get the middle of the night call from someone who wanted to enjoy the cat. I'd unlock the door, flip on the black light, put Neil Young on the turntable and go back to bed. What I'd find in the morning was anybody's guess. My writing takes Acid Cat diversions. I simply have no choice.

I have another quirk. Everyone, like the couple in my back seat, looks familiar to me. At airports, in New York City, Walmart or Shop Rite I feel like I've seen this or that person before. I don't know where that comes from but again, maybe we all have that human condition and I ain't so special.

After having read, reread, edited, edited again and taken apart my pages of notes, I'm still at a loss. Read, scan or skip. It's your choice. What happened last fall? The previous fall? Is this a true story, a vivid dream, partially true, part conjecture, out of body experience? I'm not sure. It's been an enlightening process; remembering, divining and attempting to fill in the blanks. It got my attention.

Part 1

**

1

Winter wasn't far off. You could smell it, taste it. I always enjoyed the change of season smell. It didn't last long. Either that or I just got used to it. The first whiff of either always brought with it a flood of memories. For some reason, the scent of a winter arrival brought me back to Piscataway, NJ. We'd moved to Piscataway from Plainfield, NJ in November of 1966. I was thirteen. Between late afternoon explorations of my new neighborhood and bicycle trips to and from Plainfield I was inhaling a lot of fall and winter. I guess it stuck. Spring struck the olfactory in a similar, yet different way. Maybe the warm breeze and the cold wind landed in different areas of the memory center.

But this was one of those wonderful pre-Thanksgiving nights. After spending the last twelve hours in a Lincoln MKT going back and forth between central Jersey (myth?) and Newark airport, a few minutes observing the universe from the silence of our modest patio was thoroughly grounding. Linda and I were enjoying our fifth year as residents of Delaware Crossings, a New Jersey community for the over fifty-five. I'm sixty-seven. How and when that happened, I have no idea. In the words of the late great Mickey Mantle," If I'da known I was gonna live this long I woulda' taken better care of myself." Touché', Mick.

The layout of each Delaware Crossings property was such that as small as they were, each gave a feeling of solitude and serenity. On this night, the moon was full, and the stars were stinging in their brightness. Not as striking as the night time sky my nineteen-year-old self had watched from a perch overlooking the UTEP Sun Bowl, but as a believer in the "it's all relative" school, a clear NJ night could still move and inspire me.

Tonight, seemed different. Something in the sky looked different. The bright star that was just above the bare trees was gone. The space it left was filled by the silhouette of the red barn that lived at the edge of the cornfield a few blocks away. Then the star was back. It changed color slightly and seemed to grow larger. No, it wasn't growing larger. It was getting ....closer. This was getting interesting.

2

My rose-colored glasses reminded me that life in 1950's Plainfield, NJ was close to idyllic. My parents may have differed. We shared a house at 616 Monroe Ave with our landlord, Mrs. Katz, a benevolent dictator. The proximity of my mother's parents certainly enhanced the quality of my young life. They were next door. I spent the first six years of my life at 616 and realized I could enjoy the world around me with pals of all sizes, on my own or with family. I also had an "imaginary" friend named Soupy. He was a large bear, ala a slimmer Smokey. He lived in the large radio in the living room and sported a porkpie hat, short red tie, and would join me whenever I invited him. My parents would indulge me by inviting Soupy to the dinner table, into the car etc. To this day I'm not sure what Soupy was, ET, angel, or maybe a bit of undigested potato. One day Soupy just stopped showing up. Or maybe I forgot how to invite him.

I never thought about if we were rich, poor, middle class or upper or lower. I had three meals a day, clean clothes and a warm bed. My mother would later tell me how she would sneak into my room at night to swipe a few errant pennies or a nickel for a quart of milk. Again, I never noticed.

My brother, John, was eight years older and would allow me into his clubhouse every now and then. A hard to come by invitation, indeed. The clubhouse was a cool, small backyard structure with a sliding panel on the front door which allowed the occupants to discern entry qualifications. Sometimes I'd pass muster. My sister, Marilyn, four years older than me, usually wouldn't.

The clubhouse lasted till the day after the night my brother and his pals got rousted by the South Plainfield police for "froggy giggin" at a South Plainfield lake when they should have been sleeping in their clubhouse. 'Twas a dark day for all observing the board by board dismembering of the beloved shack. A few months later my favorite swing would swing no more after falling victim to a large tree felled by the saws of my father and grandfather. The back yard was weeping.

After commandeering everyone I could to push me on my seventeen-inch bike I finally got it. I was mobile. I could go halfway around the block to join in harmless gang wars or any number of kid's games. The freedom my parents gave me is unthinkable in today's atmosphere. I was riding toward the day's action one morning when a station wagon collided with a milk truck right in front of me. That's the first time I realized the human body contains a lot of blood. Everyone survived but the thought was planted that maybe it's not so safe out here. I got over that.

I was always ducking next store to Gram and Grandpa's for a game of checkers, cards or just to enjoy the adventure of a getaway complete with cookies, soda and usually a life lesson of some sort.

My grandmother tended to be a worrier. Not a bad thing when you're a five or six-year-old kid with a touch of the wanderlust. There was a small farm, or maybe it was just an oversized back yard, that ran the length of ours and my grandparent's property. A large red barn boldly set the demarcation line between our properties and if Gram saw me headed that way the inevitable "Don't go beyond the red barn" would travel through the air and settle somewhere in my consciousness. I'd usually listen, but not always.

My grandfather had a touch of rogue in him as did his Newfoundland brothers. When Uncle Len and one-armed Uncle Jack showed up things got lively. My grandmother would kick her rosary into high gear.

When life returned to normal my grandfather and I would continue our raspberry picking and hitting lessons. He'd sit in his red metal chair in the driveway and pitch to me. I either had to hit it right at him or chase the ball. He'd let out a grunt and chuckle every time I bounced one off his belly or leg or head. It got to where I was doing less chasing and he was doing more grunting. To this day I can hit to all fields. A handy skill as I found out later. Then came the first life change.

3

My Aunt Catherine, aka Katrine, helped my parents buy their first house at 915 W Sixth St. It was just around the corner about a quarter of a mile away, but it seemed like a different world. I adapted quickly. My new twenty-inch bike got me places quicker and safer and there was no looking back.

My mother would allow me to walk the half mile or so to kindergarten at Clinton school. I would walk with my across the street neighbor, Susan, on different sides of the street. Weird. I'm not sure if she just didn't like me or that was her way of showing that she did like me. The Scott's were across the street; four girls and one boy. Mike was my pal. Two years younger. Gilly was right across the street. Two years older. Stanley was next door. One year older. There was no one right in my wheelhouse but I was pretty good at crossing ages and genders or just amusing myself. Another talent that came in handy later in life.

Once first grade started it was off to St Mary's and the Sisters of (no) Mercy. Some brutal days but I can still diagram the hell out of a sentence, compound or otherwise. The occasional year when I'd have a lay teacher was the proverbial breath of fresh air. All in all, not so bad. Lots of friends, stints as an altar boy and choir boy and duty on the "main corner" as an eighth-grade patrol boy. Cool belt.

The neighborhood years were filled with street games, baseball, bike adventures, boxing, Little Rascals type shows and eventually seeing the girls differently. Katrine's husband died. Grandpa died. Our house was cut in half as we moved downstairs and Katrine and Gram, after some renovations, move into their own apartments upstairs, great escapes for me. I still had a full basement, an attic and a huge garage to get in trouble. My father, brother and I were outnumbered. John and his pals would escape to the Social Hall and on Sundays Dad would escape to The Plainfield Rescue Squad. I'd drop in on both spots occasionally or just hang with the ladies at 915.

Walking home from school was an everyday adventure. The kids from the junior HS and HS would be walking in the opposite direction and they didn't seem to like us Catholic school kids. They were all older, bigger and the confrontations rarely went my or my friend's way. I'd either have to run, fight or talk my way out of situations. I got fairly good at navigating my way home through back yards. Then I only had to deal with the occasional dog. In the middle of all this the times they were a' changin'.

4

In November of 1963 Camelot had come crashing down on a Dallas street. By February of 1964 America was ready to breathe again. Then something extraordinary happened. It was called The British Invasion and The Beatles led the way. I was twelve and only mildly interested in the Beatles appearance on The Ed Sullivan Show that Sunday night. My sister seemed more excited than normal and even Ed and the crowd at the midtown theater seemed different, a little antsy. You'd hear these little squeals coming from the audience every now and then. Something was in the air.

John was in the army in Germany protecting us from the "Red Threat" so it was just the four of us that night. And then it happened. I had my position on the floor. The others were on the couch. I don't know when I moved but between the start of "All My Lovin" and the end of "All My Lovin" I wound up plastered against the back wall staring at the TV. My parents and sister were staring at me. We weren't in Kansas anymore.

A few months earlier on a trip to Gregory's, the premier music store in town, the sales guy and I wrangled an eighteen-dollar acoustic guitar, with felt case, out of my mother. Two dollar a week guitar lessons followed. My teacher was a folkie but Tom

Dooley and The MTA weren't really doing it for me. I'd been listening to the Motown Sound, Surf music and the pop hits of the day on AM radio. Dylan was rollin' like a stone but he wasn't quite moving me yet. The lads from Liverpool and the weekly bands that followed did. I wanted to do that!

The day after Beatles the change was all over St Mary's. It was obvious who got it and who didn't. The St Mary's Boys Choir taught me what harmony was all about and I knew enough guitar chords to get through the simple songs of the day. The streets of downtown Plainfield were in the beginning stages of Flower Power and parents were starting to be mildly concerned. TV shows and commercials had a different look. People were talking and dressing differently. At St Mary's we still had uniforms, but our hair was now down instead of up. And the girl's dresses were getting shorter. Ideas of forming bands were afoot and I was ready. Life was getting good. Then came the second life change.

5

Plainfield, NJ, like a lot of cities across the US. was having to come to grips with the issue of race. My neighborhood had changed. Stanley and I were the only originals left and the new residents still didn't seem to like our complexion. There was usually an uneasy truce but a lot of times not. Things were getting uncomfortable. My pals threw me a wonderful going away surprise party after school one day and we moved about a half hour west to Piscataway, NJ with Gram in tow. Katrine got an apartment near downtown Plainfield. I started school at Conackamack JHS in November of 1965 and adapted quickly. I fell in with a cool crew. Ron was across the street and soon got a set of drums. Rock lived down the street and played guitar. Mike was a few streets over and played bass. Finny lived behind me and became a good friend. Bruce, another former Plainfield native moved in next door and our gang was set. Other guys were scattered through the neighborhood, but this was the core.

I still had a lot of Plainfield connections, singing with the St Mary's Boys Choir and continuing the Saturday morning guitar lessons. Now trying to organize a band of some sort and hustling rides or riding my bike to and from Plainfield became my mission. My Piscataway friends mixed in with my Plainfield friends and things were cool.

At thirteen I played at my first party. It was at Billy's parents' house in Plainfield. His brother Bobby was the singer, Pete was the drummer and I was the guitar player. Girls were invited. We had to really stretch the three or four songs we knew but that didn't matter. The lesson of the night was, listen up, girls liked guitar players. By this time, I was playing a sixty-dollar Crown electric guitar through a forty-five-dollar Kay amplifier. Mom came through again. "The House of the Rising Sun," "Gloria" and "Hang on Sloopy" elevated me. And after that night I had my first girlfriend. Debbie was also a guitar player. And better than me.

I was fading out of Plainfield and into Piscataway. Junior HS and High School always found me in one kind of band or another; The Plague, Society's Child and The Best of General Milz to name a few. Music had become a nice source of weekend income.

Ron went on to play drums with The Penetrators, one of the premier Jersey bands of the day. I did a lot of gigs with Ronnie for several years in a variety of different bands. He could always be relied on as a last-minute fill in and could play any style, any time. By the mid-eighties he'd given up drumming and wrangling a drum kit for him as needed was par for the musical course. On one gig he was using an old snare drum of mine that was being held together by a shoelace. Every few songs he'd have to stop for a quick spot repair. In his 70's heyday one of his bands opened for Ozzy at the Sunshine Inn in Asbury Park. Ron got me backstage and brought the house down with a killer drum solo. He was a talented guy. I gave him his first drum lesson and he passed me by in about a week and a half. I gave him his first guitar lesson and after about a year we were neck and neck. Some years later when my band Freewheelin' needed a fill in for our laid-up fiddler, Ronnie filled in on harmonica. He practiced all week and nailed it. He was one of those guys who didn't realize how talented he was. I was the best man at his wedding, and he was one of my best pals in life. He moved to Florida and left this earth in the early nineties. And so, it goes.

Piscataway life hit its stride. Marilyn went to college and soon got married. Johnny came home, got married and started living life. My father had a debilitating stroke when I was seventeen and life got a lot more difficult for mom. Katrine would drive Dad to rehab twice a week and Gram was getting "forgetful." I'd had a pleasant enough life playing music, surfing down the Jersey shore, lots of neighborhood baseball and football games, beer blasts, sneaking into Rutgers frat parties and learning how to deal with the opposite sex. But by my senior year I was ready for a change. Mom bought me a suitcase for graduation, co-signed a thousand-dollar loan and in the fall of 1970 gave me a lift to Newark airport. I was off to UTEP, The University of Texas at El Paso. A week later my neighbor and best pal, Bruce, appeared in my dorm to also begin college life.

There I found that everyone was escaping life in their various homes and, like me, looking for something. The guys I met who were El Paso natives wanted to come to NJ, NY, the east coast...... away from home! That was an interesting year. Lots of psychedelics, hikes around the southwest desert and mountains, concerts, an Easter break in the hills of Laurel Canyon, Calif, sneaking girls into dorm rooms and a Christmas break drive back to NJ in a Toyota with a missing back windshield. We broke down in Harrisburg, PA. Bruce's girlfriend Diane drove out to pick us up. We were a little nervous about the "presents" we were bringing back but all was well, and a good time was had by all. Bruce opted out of a second semester but did come out for an extended visit. An increase in tuition for out of state students the following year made for an easy decision. Back to Jersey.

6

I spent the next year and a half or so at loose ends. I picked up some credits at Trenton State College while picking up some cash working in the cafeteria. The occasional steak sometimes wound up coming home with me. Home was now an apartment across the river in Pennsylvania that I shared with two high school pals, one a former band mate. Then

13

followed a year at Middlesex County College and working nights at UPS with Mike and Bruce. The boss took a shine to me and I got the plum job of driving the little car around the warehouse picking up package carts over here and dropping them off over there. I made sure to give the boys a beep every time I rode past them as they loaded up the trucks.

The next year I got a full-time job at Brunswick, the sports equipment guys. At lunch we'd grab a football or a baseball and a couple of gloves and while away forty-five minutes. I had a low lottery number and with no college deferment thought there was a good chance I'd be getting drafted. Guys I knew coming back from Vietnam convinced me not to enlist so I decided to leave it up to the fates. The fates decided I wouldn't be going, one of my life's regrets. A few months later brought a week in the hospital with pneumonia That was a wakeup call. Not for long.

I came out of the hospital unemployed but landed a cool gig as a security guard for Wells Fargo. My assignment was at an empty Union Steel warehouse in Piscataway. The little air-conditioned guard house was my home. I worked a lot of hours there, sometimes three shifts in a row. The boys would come visit packing guitars and my former musical life was getting a kick start. Seven years after The Plague rocked Conackamack JHS we were getting the band back together. I had an epiphany in a music store one night and switched to bass. I was home. Mike switched to guitar and Rock, Ron, Mike and I started The Wichita Straw Band. We added Joe on guitar and Lew on fiddle and had a good time on the local bar scene and college pubs. Mike decided to pursue higher learning and after a few false starts with female singers, Freewheelin' was born.

My girlfriend at the time decided to move to Colorado. I rode out on the back of a buddy's Harley for a visit. It was November and it rained from Jersey to St Louis. He went on to the Snake River Canyon for the Evel Knievel debacle. After a short Denver visit, I flew home and that was that. I was at a crossroads. An old high school friend offered me a job at the company where he was the operations manager. Meanwhile Freewheelin' was hitting its stride. But first Rock and I snuck in a hell ride to Denver in his MG Midget to once again visit the ex-girlfriend. The first gas station we hit west of the Mississippi called for a Coors stop. At that time Coors wasn't available on the East Coast. Our arrival was delayed by about a day.

On our return home from the Colorado hell ride we all went full in with Freewheelin' and had a rather good five-year run. Small concerts, plenty of bar work and free studio time at Tony Camillo's Venture Sounds to record original music. The Venture Sounds guys worked the door at a club we played regularly and got us in. Gladys Knight had just finished recording Midnight Train to Georgia there and now we were up.

We met with Tony in his white shag office. The whole scene was the epitome of struggling band meets record producer. Tony was very generous giving us carte blanche and sending us off with the words, "Just do whatever it takes to get the music rollin'," or something like that. We had free studio time in the nicest studio I've been in before or since, complete with pro engineers. I wish we could have seen the opportunity that was ours for the taking. "The saddest words of voice or pen are those that say, what might have been."

Before we could really get rolling Freewheelin' ended its run. No big scene just ran out of steam. Our last gig was at The Red Fox Inn in New Brunswick and I assumed that was probably the end of my music career. At the end of the night Joy approached me and said their band Caligula was reforming and needed a bass player. Reality would have to wait.

Jump to some years later and I was once again called upon to be a best man. Rock had a whammer jammer of a wedding. My next book will be about the fall of the marriage, and the fall of Rock, my brother from another mother. His liver finally screamed, "No mas!" and about a year and a half ago he quietly departed. And so, it goes, again.

The ten years post Freewheelin' saw hundreds of gigs with different Jersey bands, some more successful than others; Caligula, Sundown, Walking Wounded, Freight Line, The Wyatt Brothers and The Firecreek Band to name a few. A two-month stint with The Firecreek Band in Bermuda, '83 brought the end of full-time music.

7

On our return to Jersey the three of us got day gigs while continuing band gigs at night. On off nights I was attempting to finish that pesky English degree at Rutgers. It was a busy time. The debilitating stroke my father'd had years earlier set the stage for a final stroke on New Year's Eve of '81. He'd had his first one on Easter. I'm always a little nervous around holidays.

My mother had been fighting, and losing, a battle with Wegners Granular Mytosis; a circulatory disease that eventually resulted in amputation of both legs. She fought the hell out of it but on New Year's Day 1990 a stroke, then a heart attack a few days later, sent her on her way. She's written up in a few medical journals. She'd have liked that. She had a good ten year run of travel, friends and the discovery of a talent for painting. She always encouraged me but thought I'd eventually get over my music habit. That never happened. I owe her a lot.

Post Bermuda gig I got a job as a courier for a tape storage facility and was eventually offered an operations manager position at a sister company. After five years it just didn't fit. I didn't, and never would, have the corporate makeup. I continued with a martial arts program that I'd started a few years earlier and earned a first-degree black belt while working at a NJ Tae Kwon Do school. That tenure ended after I moved out to Hunterdon County, NJ with my soon to be wife, Donna. A few years later, after a two-month solo cross-country odyssey, we got married in the summer of '93.

Shortly thereafter I became a limo driver/office guy as well as a Thurs morning DJ at WDVR FM in Sergeantsville, NJ. Band gigs continued, a home recorded cd got released and I embarked on a solo career as a guitar/singer. The band scene was dying out. People that went to see bands weren't staying out late and club owners couldn't afford to pay full bands anymore. What once was a five-piece band evolved into two guys and a drum machine. And so, it goes, and continues to go. I rarely get a chance to play bass anymore but guitar opportunities are plentiful.

I returned to Bermuda twice, went to the Cayman Islands once, walked a marathon in Northern

California, skydived (dove?) last year and took a hell ride to Cleveland's Rock and Roll Hall of Fame with one of my Firecreek/Sundown buddies. Tom was slowly fading from colon cancer and the effects of his "treatments." We did a few more gigs together but this was to be our last hurrah. He left us about a year later but not before we got to see Cleveland rock. Post-divorce I had two serious relationships that just didn't pan out. Lovely, beautiful women both but was not to be. I was lucky to find another beautiful lady with an equally beautiful heart and here we are at Delaware Crossings, a community for the over fifty-five.

Linda's had her own challenges. Her daughter Carrie had complications during childbirth and lost ninety percent of her small intestine. It was an extremely challenging couple of weeks. Funeral arrangements were silently being contemplated. Carrie survived, received and lost another small intestine and as of this writing is doing well as a single mom and lives a few miles away with her two kids. I've inherited four grown children and ten grandchildren and get togethers for a big kid like me are always a blast. I'm afraid I'm an instigator. I have a second home in "time outs."

On my side I'm an uncle five times over and a great uncle nine times over. Along with the earlier mentioned regret of no military service, never having children of my own and falling short of a college degree are two more life regrets. One I'm still determined to fulfill and the other just ain't happenin'. You decide which is which. That's the "Readers Digest" version of life to date. Now things get kinda weird.

Part 2

**

1

The bright star that was just above the bare trees was gone. The space it left was filled by the silhouette of the red barn that lived at the edge of the cornfield a few blocks away. Then the star was back. It changed color slightly and seemed to grow larger. No, it wasn't growing larger. It was getting.........closer. This was getting interesting. I thought I heard, or maybe felt, a slight "whoosh," as if I'd entered an airtight room and someone pulled the door shut. My ears popped and I thought for a second that I might pass out. I guess that's my reaction when I see something that doesn't fit into my reality. I was a little wobbly as that surreal feeling of "this can't be happening" washed over me. But here it was.

The star of a few seconds earlier was now a bright egg resting on or slightly above my lawn, maybe twenty-five or thirty feet from me. It slowly dimmed and I realized it had been making a low melodic hum as now there was silence. The night had never seemed so silent as the egg brightened and dimmed, brightened and dimmed as if a beating heart. Then it dimmed, dimmed and dimmed. Then stopped. No sound. No light. If not for the soft glow of the late Indian summer moon it would have faded into the shadows of the tree line. Someone had shut 'er down!

2

I'd imagined this scenario in my head a number of times, probably like many of you. Would I run? Faint? Engage? I've talked to people who thought we were alone in the universe. My brother is one of those people. The thought that we could possibly be alone was a little frightening, lonely, and to me, just not possible. The Drake equation and Fermi Paradox notwithstanding, (in short, one pro, one con) once you remind the other guy of the amount of stars in our own Milky Way galaxy (200 - 400 billion and counting) and the number of galaxies in the known universe (2 trillion and counting) and note that planets, which had not been seen till recently, now seem to be the norm around stars/suns, you'd get that nod of reluctant possibility.

To date about twenty-five hundred planets have been discovered outside our solar system by the Kepler Telescope. Kepler has found, as of this writing, thirty plus potentially habitable planets within its extremely limited line of vision. That means they're located in the "Goldilocks Zone," far enough from, yet close enough to their sun to possibly have water and an atmosphere. Does that mean life? Maybe, but probably not. Earth had water and an atmosphere long before the primordial ooze produced anything, we could call life. But look at us now!! Even my own conservative, doubtful, "ya gotta show me" brother will concede the remote possibility that maybe.........

Hearkening back to Mr. Haldane's theory, I'm open to all possibilities. Maybe we ARE in a computer simulation. Maybe we ARE one of countless universes and timelines. Or, like one of my college buddies (and Professor Donald Sutherland in "Animal House") put forth, maybe our universe IS in the fingernail of a giant. Can you prove it's not?

Which brings me back to my Delaware Crossings backyard on that clear, brisk, weird fall night. I had a feeling I was about to get one or two answers to some ancient questions. I stood still, watching, listening. Ok. So, run wasn't happening. It seemed I wasn't about to faint, so far. Engage? I was kind of waiting, almost but not quite hoping, to wake up in my bed. I looked around as if to confirm that this egglike anomaly and I were here, now. Indeed I, and it, was. It had been about thirty seconds since I realized this was no star, and watched its descent and landing, till now. The decision to exercise my third option, engage, was about to be taken out of my hands.

3

I was, of course, thinking purely extrateresstrially. But the realization struck me of the distinct possibility that this was a Nasa or Military aircraft off course, or maybe an errant pilot needing a restroom or just looking to amaze the local gentry. I have to say that thought took a little of the wind out of my sails. What I saw approaching immediately reinflated them. I hadn't noticed any kind of door or window opening but somehow, someone had exited and was undoubtedly coming toward me.

My options disappeared as I tried to wrap my head around what was standing directly in front of me. Well, how 'bout that! I was still here. But I was fairly sure I wouldn't be able to speak as my throat was about as dry as it had ever been.

I had a flashback to a junior year late August football double session. My mouth had been so dry that when I tried to spit all that came out was a kind of brown dust. We were about to run a twenty-three dive which meant I'd be getting the ball, but in the middle of the count our quarterback turned around and threw up. Oh good, a break. That's how dry my throat seemed on this strange, strange evening.

Here we were. Face to face. Many nights I'd stood out on this slab of cement outside my back door waiting for Molly to complete her nightly ritual or pull up a chair to simply enjoy the nighttime universe. I never knew what I was looking at but the sight always evoked feelings; feelings of how small and insignificant we really were and how those life stresses that seemed so overwhelming earlier in the day weren't all that important after all. We're only here for a cosmic heartbeat and then what? On more than one occasion I'd thrown out an invitation to whoever might be listening that they were welcome to drop in. Let's meet. That old chestnut about being careful what you wished for was slapping me in the face.

The brain's an amazing computer. Those few thoughts raced through my head in about a second and a half ending in a kind of crazy, short burst of dry, raspy laughter. Time to acknowledge the situation. What to say? My guest stepped up. "It's time we meet," he said. The voice was masculine, friendly and I thought I detected a slight British accent. I put out my hand in what I assumed was the universal sign of "Nice to meetcha" and when there was obviously no reaction simply said, "Welcome." He reached out and held my wrist, which was still extended, for just a second then released. Done. I've had some interesting bro handshakes over the years but that was odd. I realized I had a huge grin on my face and hoped our stretching of lips and display of teeth wasn't a sign of aggression as in some realms of the animal kingdom.

I don't know what I expected. A prescient bug like creature? ET? A floating head? I was staring at something remarkably familiar. Us. He was exactly my height; five feet nine, give or take the shrinking of age and was very slim but with longer arms and hands. The head was oblong.... egglike, and seemed too big for its spindly body. I realized in a second that the head was encased in a form fitting helmet of some kind. It was clear all around and afforded me a good look at the features. Large black eyes. Or maybe they looked large in contrast to the tiny nose. The nose was a small hump with two pinoles. But the eyes were a deep black, a large black or dark pupil with a small white rim. What threw me off immediately was that they didn't blink in unison. They each had a life of their own. Why would nature do that? I'd never know. I forgot to ask.

Remember Pat Paulsen? He was a regular on the Smothers Brothers TV show back in the day. During one season he comically entered the then current presidential race. His speeches would be semi obviously run split screen and as a result his blinking would be out of sync. The seriousness of his demeanor combined with the blinking was comic entertainment at its most yuk filled. So, I started to chuckle at my new friend's eye disparity. I thought that maybe it was intentional. Maybe going into a routine was their ice breaker. I thought, "Well, I'll break into some armpit farts." I didn't, stopped chuckling and decided for some reason this was the way he rolled, and I shouldn't be rude. But it looked strange. Google Pat Paulsen/Smothers Brothers/ blinking or something like that. The mouth was smaller and more square than ours but had obvious small lips and descended into a long, angular chin. Again, I thought, why? And again, never asked. I observed that the eyes, while blinking independently would stay closed for a period where just one eye would be open for a second or two, kind of comical and a little disconcerting. Just to confuse things sometimes they would blink together then go into the Pat Paulsen thing. I got used to it quickly. There were no discernible eyebrows and the forehead seemed to come to a V shape at the top ending at a visible hair line. I realized that the helmet was oblong because the head was oblong. Genius! I couldn't see any ears from this angle and because of the dark, but a slight bulge on both sides of the head gear gave an impression of something there. All in all, the physical alien rendering that we've become accustomed to was close. But there was more humanity to this guy. I won't say you wouldn't look at him twice if you saw him walking down the street but maybe he could get away with it. The offbeat blinking may get a look or two.

Seinfeld does a bit where he imagines the clothing of the future would be a one piece stretch ensemble with a lightning bolt across the front. This is what we'll all agree on and it takes the anxiety of "What am I gonna wear today?" out of the morning equation. I prefer uniforms. St Mary's had uniforms. Some bands I was in had uniforms. As a limo driver a black suit, white shirt and red tie is the uniform. Makes life easy. Especially for a guy like me who has no fashion sense. I guess this is where we wind up because that's what my guest was wearing; a dark one-piece wet suit like thing with, indeed, a lightning bolt, or something akin to a lightning bolt on the upper right chest. Jerry was right. The suit seemed to drop right into the shoes like a kid's pajamas and looked extremely comfortable. To this point maybe five seconds had passed since I'd said my welcome and as we checked each other out I suspected I was not the first human he'd seen but I couldn't be sure of that.

He said, "We'd like to get to know you" and motioned to his vessel. To my astonishment I didn't hear this with my ears but in my head. Wow! Telepathy is the wave of the future. Makes sense. But why a British accent? Why not New York or Memphis.

Forgot to ask. I felt someone behind me and there were Linda and Molly. She was whiter than normal, Linda, that is. Molly seemed disinterested.

"I have to go," I said, still unsure if I could move. She said," Teeeeddd" .....very softly and seemed to be visibly shaking. I turned to the dude and said, "I'll be back, right?" He said.... thought, "Shortly. We have some things you should see." Well, this was one of those life moments. I walked back to Linda, gave her a hug and a kiss and with a look of what the hell am I doing, turned back and followed my new friend who was walking back to his craft. There was no way I couldn't.

4

I was in the middle of the granddaddy of out of body experiences. Surreal doesn't quite say it. This can't be happening! And yet....it was. As we got close to the "egg" I didn't see an entrance or door of any kind. My guide walked up to and through the side of the craft. He was outside. Then he was inside. I just kept walking, right on his heels and passed through what seemed like a gelatinous curtain. I was in. Two things immediately got my attention. From the outside the egg appeared opaque. From the inside it was a 360-degree window, like one of those two-way mirrors you see in police interrogation rooms. Somehow the floor was a square, stable surface, but also clear. And we were not alone. There was another being that looked a lot like my guy and was dressed similarly. The inside was softly and comfortably lit so that the outside was still clearly visible, and I noticed that their "uniforms" were dark but different shades. They also appeared more human in this environment. I could see that the helmet they wore was an oblong, but the head was more rounded. They also appeared very pale and hair was visible. My host was a blonde and the new guy appeared to have darker, somewhat curly hair. They were both looking down at an iPad type device that Curly was working. He looked up at me, put down the pad and extended his arm. He was smiling, I think. We did the wrist shake thing and I "heard" him say, "This is exciting, isn't it? "I said, "You've done this before?"

"It's been a while," he said. I asked what their names were, what I should call them, and they replied with sounds I couldn't pronounce on my best day. It was something so foreign I can't really compare it to anything except maybe the clicking that some African cultures use but with a pitch of some kind. Summoning my R & B memories, I decided to call them Sam and Dave, Curly being Dave. They communicated by thought but would also speak out loud. The language was not unpleasant to the human ear. The tenor of their voice was mellow; low and soothing in a strange vibratory way.

The inside of the egg was bare except for a bar that ran all the way around the wall at roughly a four-foot height. It looked like a high-quality wood, grain and all but it probably wasn't. Dave put down the pad, communicated with Sam, looked in my direction and said, "Ready?" I was sure I was either going to have a heart attack or a stroke, or both, but I nodded. Yes. I was ready.

5

I was trying to put my finger on the aroma within the craft. It was pleasant, heavy and reminiscent of...something. It came to me. My grandfather died when I was in the second grade. My first visit to a funeral home followed shortly thereafter. The floral aroma upon entering Higgin's Home for Funerals in Plainfield, NJ was, to say the least, pungent, but pleasant. I've always believed that the sense of smell is the strongest of the emotional triggers. I can't walk into a flower shop or even smell a flowery bouquet without being thrown back for just a second or two to Higgins Home for Funerals.

The ensuing trips to Higgins through the years and to other funeral homes always bring me back to my grandfather's time in the large, flowery family business at West Eighth St in Plainfield. One of my classmates was a Higgins. There were fourteen of them. My brother and sister also had a Higgins for a classmate. Most grades did. Mine had a part time gig at the funeral home washing hair for the "clients." I remember asking her about the creep factor and she said, "Well, it doesn't matter if you get soap in their eyes." True dat.

The recognition of the aroma within the room and its familiarity in the midst of all this unfamiliarity was comforting. I'd been leaning on the circular bar and suddenly found myself behind it secured in a kind of invisible clear force. It seemed as if I'd been gently grabbed. It felt safe but somehow not confining at all. Sam and Dave were in their own areas behind the bar. We were spaced at an equal distance within the egg and probably could have fit three or four more people comfortably. The dim light inside dimmed even more and I noticed light on the outside perimeter of our vessel. Sam and Dave were looking at me and there was a moment of stillness, anticipation. It was like that moment right before the pitcher delivers the ball and all the players are tensed and poised. Anything can happen in those next few seconds.

I felt just the slightest sensation of movement, like a modern, smooth running elevator. I was excited for the slow hot air balloon like rise over my home and neighborhood and seeing the local hotspots from the "bird's eye view." That was not to be. I caught a flash of a red barn and imagined I'd heard my grandmother's earlier warnings. Our craft made a sweeping left bank and within seven or eight seconds, too quick to fully comprehend, I looked up and out and saw a panorama of the earth. The lights of New York bled into my New Jersey home and the sight literally took my breath away. Sam and Dave were looking at me and I believe they were enjoying the look of amazement on my face. That was quick, no sensation of movement. We seemed to stop but there was really no way to tell. I was awed by the sight. I heard the words, "Behold your home." I thought, "How biblical."

I don't know if they heard my inner reply or not, but this moment needed a soundtrack. Not a "Star Wars" or even a "2001, A Space Odyssey" but something classy, classical, overwhelming and maybe a little dark. No, not dark. I don't know. But it needed something. The earth was, simply put, stunningly beautiful. I felt light from behind me and there was our old familiar friend, the Moon, brighter and clearer than I'd ever seen it. I've enjoyed the moon from several different heights and Earth locations, but this was certainly the most magnificent. That's it. Beethoven's "Moonlight Sonata" would have to be the soundtrack for this moment.

The silence was deafening. Maybe no soundtrack was necessary. For the movie, maybe, but in this moment, none needed. My mates were being perfect first-time hosts, allowing me to let this wash over me. I think they knew/sensed what I was feeling and just let the moment linger. As a bonus the already dim light inside went dark and the "blackness of space" had new meaning. Earth looked so fragile and helpless in the black void. It was getting smaller. We were moving and now I was observing Mother Earth from the "Dark Side of The Moon." (cue the "Floyd") We hung there with the Moon seeming close enough to touch and the Earth just beyond. I was thinking that the side we see from Earth is much more interesting. If they brought me home, dropped me off and said, "It's a start," that that would have been more than enough. This was just the beginning.

6

Direction was meaningless to me, but I got the impression I was being taken on a tour of our neighborhood. My immediate neighborhood, Moon and Earth, were fading rapidly. Next stop? The stars started to appear as rain running down a windowpane, but horizontally. It was like when The Enterprise hits impulse power and the stars look like…. this. So far Star Trek was right on point with the uniforms, iPad, liquid stars etc. We'll see from here. I had a slight elevator stopping feeling in my stomach and the stars were solid once again. I turned around and put my hands up on the "glass" like a kid at the Macy's Christmas window. There was a slight vertigo but at this point I was all in and assumed I was in good hands with these guys. There was a dot in front of me that was getting larger, quickly. We'd slowed but that was a relative term. About two or three minutes had passed and I recognized the ball in front of us. The red planet, Mars. I was trying, and had to keep reminding myself, to remember everything, sights, sounds, feelings, colors, smells.

I had an Art Appreciation class during my tenure at Rutgers night school. It was a fascinating course with an engaging professor. After working all day, I really didn't feel like concentrating and taking notes. I just wanted to kick back and listen, enjoy the lecture. But I couldn't. I even dropped in on her class periodically so I could just enjoy. That's where I was on this journey. I was really trying to pay attention. So far so good. Mars! I was thinking about the effort and cost it takes our Nasa rockets to just escape Earth's hold and then the time, expense and effort to get to the space station, moon or here.

Watching the Insight and Rover missions to Mars were/are very cool and exciting but slow. I want to be everywhere now! I'm sure that's the way the gang in Mission Control feels, too. That is one smart, impressive group. I had a brief pang of guilt as I considered who should probably be here in my place. That passed. But these baby steps into the universe are necessary. It's the only way. Sam and Dave's predecessors must have gone through a similar growing process. But here we were, Earth to Mars in under five minutes. Or was time somehow being bent or skewed? The red planet was indeed red and more stunning than any pictures.

I flashed on a Bermuda memory. The Bermudian water is a color blue that must be seen live. Pictures don't do it justice. I remember it. Many afternoons I sat on the rocks overlooking the ocean at Horseshoe Bay. Pink sand. Spectacular water. Colorful reef inhabitants lazily floating. I remember thinking at the time, this will end soon. Keep this feeling, this picture. I have.

I've usually been able to recognize "moments." Sometimes you have to create them. Turn off the radio, tv, iPad, phone and just dream. I know. Scary. My job as a limo driver affords me many opportunities to pull over by a lake, stream, scenic overlook or my favorite, a manicured baseball field and turn off and chill out. Breathe. It's an absolutely necessary part of my day. Now I must remember, really remember, this. I will. I did, for as long as I could.

I was thinking I'd like to get closer. I wasn't sure how this telepathy thing worked. Could Sam and Dave read everything I was thinking, or did I have to direct a question or thought directly to them? Could they read through the clutter and zero in on the important stuff? I'd find out but now we were heading on a crash course into Mars. I watched and trusted. We came sliding in and eased into a slow peruse about fifty yards above the surface. This was just too freakin' cool! I don't know how the mass of questions and thoughts must have sounded but Sam said, out loud, "Millions of years ago this was once like your earth."

"A civilization?" I said.

"No", he said. "There was abundant life, but nothing you'd recognize as life. It all got blown away before it could take hold." I didn't understand. I don't think that's actually what he said but that's the way I heard it, or at least interpreted it. Before I could follow up with the myriad of questions that were floating around in my head, we were soaring over a gorgeous mountain range into a breathtaking Martian sunset. I wanted to find the Opportunity Rover or Insight, take a selfie and call Nasa from there. I was in a position to save them a lot of time and effort. But

I didn't want to push any kind of agenda. I was strictly along for the ride. And I thought things were probably going to pick up for humankind exponentially once I got back. Got back. Wow. Home. That just dawned on me. What was the plan there? Again. Just be a good guest. Shut up and take it in. Lead on.

7

We picked up speed and arced up into the blackness once again. Quickly! I had no idea how fast we were traveling but again the stars were melting. The fellas took turns appearing to control our craft with the iPad device which seemed to stay wherever whoever had it let it go. It didn't float like we're used to seeing objects float on the International Space Station but seemed to remain solidly in place until it was grabbed again. It looked very odd, like it was being held by invisible Velcro. More questions.

I assumed the atmosphere inside the egg was adjusted for me. Besides the flowery aroma, I was breathing, apparently, air. Sam and Dave kept their helmets on. They were very accommodating. We slowed and a colorful dot was appearing on our left. It was getting larger, LARGER...in a hurry.

We stopped. I think. The dot on Jupiter was immense and appeared to be moving. The vastness of the sight before me was staggering. When I was a kid,

I had a book that tried to describe the relation of objects to each other. How big is big? How small is small? The ant compared to the blue whale. I realized I wasn't breathing and let out a large exhale. How big is big? It was in front of me!

Again, distance was impossible for me to judge but Jupiter appeared to me as Earth appears from the International Space Station. I can stare at that shot of Earth on the NASA channel for, well, a few minutes. How spoiled we've gotten. We just take the brilliance of our scientists, engineers, biologists, botanists etc. for granted. I remember watching NASA during the Insight pre landing and the list of all the things that had to go right and could possibly go wrong. It all worked. Perfectly. As satisfying as that must have been for the NASA gang, we are the veritable slugs inching our way along the cosmic path. But that's the way it has to be. Or does it?

I thought, "Man, I'd like to land there," and immediately remembered, though I'm merely an interested space geek, that Jupiter's a big ball of gas and there'd be no landing. Sam and Dave didn't acknowledge as we began a swoop down through and along the upper atmosphere. We got a little lower and things seemed to be thickening. I heard, "Listen." We stopped. It was as if a window was opened and the sound and presence of wind was rushing through our egg. I thought I almost heard a wind chime effect. I certainly felt a cold wind on my arm and watched goose bumps arrive. Explanation? I have none. Up, up and away.

How much time had passed, I'm not sure. I hoped I'd be able to see, and before I finished, a dot appeared far, far out. Rings were barely visible. I took this moment to ask what their mode was of moving through the cosmos at such fantastic speeds. Dave looked directly at me and spoke in a voice that sounded similar to Sam's and said," We use a combination of sailing on solar winds, the magnetic push and pull of individual stars and galactic pathways."

"Wormholes," I asked?

"No," he said, "but areas of space where the pace of travel is exponentially increased allowing greater distances to be traveled quickly." I was thinking about a European car going sixty-five miles an hour then jumping onto the Autobahn and cranking it up to one twenty. Sam and Dave were both looking at me and.... grinning? I think I got the concept but the physics of it I wouldn't/couldn't touch.

8

In college I always did a surprisingly good job of avoiding the math and science buildings. They were anathema to me. And finally, I get to use that word in the perfect context. I could write papers all day, even had a sideline in College writing papers for fellow procrastinators. The content may have been sketchy, but I could fill pages.

My brother, sister and I were always told that we were a solid C family and that math and science were not our strong suit. That's probably not a good thing to tell kids, true or not, but in our case, it became a self-fulfilling prophecy. It was only slightly disheartening going into an Algebra or Geometry class knowing the frustrating challenges ahead only to be followed by the unavoidable, and welcome, C at the end. I squeaked through my first Geometry course after a stint in summer school and went onto Geometry Two. I was still lost. I asked my teacher if he'd consider giving me a little help. I'll always appreciate Mr. Koersten for patiently sitting with me after school and painstakingly going through proofs, even earlier ones which I still didn't understand. I didn't know what we were trying to prove, why we were trying to prove it or what difference it made particularly when important things like preparations for a huge concert up in Woodstock, NY, which would be moved to Bethel, NY, were getting underway! But then....one day....... Euclid and I became one. The light went on. I got it! I felt like saying, "Well, why the hell didn't you say so in the first place?" I didn't say that. Mr. Koersten was jubilant. We went through the first Geometry book that I struggled with and breezed. The current subject matter was still challenging but I got it. And if I hadn't been playing gigs on weekends, smoking pot, and chasing girls I probably, with a minimum of effort, could have aced it. But we were a solid C family and math and science were not our strong suit. I'm afraid I couldn't avoid a B. I made up for it in ensuing math courses of which there were few.

I had a few Saturnian facts in my head. Wikipedia? Saturn is about nine hundred million miles from the sun, depending on the time of year, takes almost thirty years to travel around the sun, and is one hundred times more massive than Earth. Nine Earth's could span Saturn's diameter and if a large enough body of water could be found Saturn would float. More moons than you could shake a stick at, some with the possibility of life. I should have asked. I didn't. But those rings. Who came up with that? Saturn appeared as if looking at the moon from Earth, on a spectacularly clear night. Descriptions had to be made on the fly and they just don't tell the whole story but I'm trying. I knew we were heading out. Out! Uranus (still makes me laugh), Neptune and poor old Pluto. Then into Voyager territory.

Now Saturn filled the void in front of us. Not like Jupiter but still over whelming. We were moving as small and large chunks of rock went whizzing by. We were passing through the rings of Saturn. A misstep could end our adventure prematurely. Trust. We stopped next to a chunk that was the size of a small house and they all seemed to be moving. On past the rings and we hung over the surface of Saturn. I'm guessing a few hundred miles but who knew? My eyes were starting to hurt from being open so wide. Wide eyed is a real thing. I made a conscious effort to blink a few times and relax the old orbs. Better. Saturn had distinctive bands of what I assumed were clouds. They each had defined borders. Again, they said, "Listen." I heard a hum. A hum! A cosmic hum! As I listened, I could hear four or five distinct sounds that occasionally merged into a harmony of a kind. It was angelic. "The wind colliding with space," I heard from across the egg. A feeling came over me and I was on the brink of crying. I was so happy. The music was everywhere. I was so proud of us for recognizing and harnessing the beauty of music. It was real. It was celestial. It was all around us. It was ancient. From cave people pounding out a rhythm on logs and rocks to Mozart to the Sex Pistols, we got it. Some more than others but we got it. A touch of melancholy came over me as I knew I should have worked harder at what I thought was my meager gift. But music was math and I was still a solid C student.

9

The guys were scanning the "iPad" and speaking to someone. Then they put the pedal to the metal. Saturn was disappearing and the stars were once again liquid. We stayed on this course for about ten minutes then slowed, slowed, slowed to a stop. The stars were once again solid. I asked if we were still in my galaxy and they said we wouldn't be going beyond that. Which made me wonder how far could they, had they, gone? I hadn't thought of it before, but I suddenly blurted out, "Where are you from?" They both looked up and seemed a little surprised that I was interested. Where were my manners? I was nothing BUT interested.

Dave pointed directly over our tiny star and said, "Two stars to the right of your sun. Barnard's Star. (I think that sounded familiar. Info overload.) We come from a system with twelve planets. Ours is the only life there, the only original life We have settlers on one of our moons. But ours is the only planet where life has naturally evolved yet." The "yet" hung there. I'd never considered that. If someone cruised by Earth two billion years after the planet had started evolving, the "no life yet" moniker would have applied.

The oldest human, Lucy, was, if I remember, about three to four million years old. Lucy's got some 'splainin' to do. How far we've come.

Sam and Dave came out from behind the barrier and motioned for me to do the same. We weren't weightless apparently, but I felt decidedly lighter, freer. I was moving around and stretching but space was limited. A few steps and I'd be across the egg and in their way. This seemed to be a craft designed for temporary jaunts, if you could call a trip across and out of the solar system a temporary jaunt. No food. No bathroom, both of which I'd be needing soon. How long had I been gone? About forty-five minutes? How long in real time? Was this real time? When I returned would everyone I know have aged? Was Einstein right, as *Close Encounters of the Third Kind* had postulated? That nagging thought of be careful what you wish for was floating around again. C'mon, man. Sit back. Relax. Enjoy the ride.

Sam and Dave took their helmets off. Dave's hair wasn't curly and dark but blondish like Sam's. Their heads appeared round in their helmets but were slightly more angular, very human. They'd still elicit a double take on the street, but, human. The dark curls on Dave's head had been a covering of some kind. I don't know where it appeared from, but Sam gave me a uniform and a helmet, all one piece. He asked me if I'd like to take a walk in space. My words, not his. I would hear what they were saying but then it would be translated into thoughts I could understand. This wasn't even a conscious thing. It just happened.

There seemed to be an invisible fluid curtain between us much like the walls of the egg and we seemed to each have our own atmospheres. Of course, I had to take my clothes off to put the uniform on. That felt a little odd, but they didn't seem to care. It went on easily like a well-worn wetsuit. It brought me back to Long Beach Island and struggling in and out of sandy wetsuits. Something familiar. It was open all the way down the right side and I stepped in. It was like a onesie for adults, feet and all. I pulled the helmet over my head and everything seemed to snap into place. My helmet was a little different. I got a faint glimpse of myself in the window of the egg. I looked like one of the little aliens with the big eyes and no features. I had to think about that. Had we been having close encounters with this uniform?

Dave walked over into my area and felt around the suit. "OK "he asked? I nodded and at that a section of the circular interior barrier opened, as I guess it had done when we first entered, and Dave led me to the edge of the floor. I'd gone skydiving a couple of years ago and I had a feeling I was…. yup…. nudged through the "wall" and out into space. I was moving further away. The egg, which was already tiny was disappearing. I had a momentary feeling of panic but heard a familiar voice say, "Don't worry. It's alright. Enjoy this experience. We'll be back." Again, those weren't the words I heard but that was the message that was conveyed. And then they were gone.

10

Wow! Alone doesn't say it. Brilliant. Frightening. God. I didn't know, had no idea, where I was. Somewhere between stars and well outside our solar system. In the middle of the blackest of black with a view of distant stars as thick as any planetarium roof had ever displayed. There was no awareness of up or down, but I did have a sense of moving. I could hear blood circulating through my body, my heart beating and the old familiar sound of the tinnitus that had followed me since my days of playing rock and roll six nights a week.

We really had abused our ears. I remember leaving many concerts with a ringing in my ears that could last well into the next day. My favorite band practice position was sitting on the floor with my back against my Fender Bassman amp which would be turned up to an unnecessary, but fun, level. I never considered the ramifications. Me and Pete Townsend, spokesman for the tinnitus community never considered the ramifications. Tinnitus is described as the perception of noise or a ringing in the ears. I'm one of the lucky ones. My tinnitus, when it cranks up, sounds like crickets or cicadas singing their summertime song. Other people have to put up with annoying, whining, high pitched sounds. Mine's kind of pleasant. Many's the summer night Linda and I would sit out back, where this adventure started, and enjoy the summer evening. I was told on more than one occasion that the sounds of the woods I was enjoying weren't really there. I enjoyed them anyway.

Like the feeling of rolling out of an airplane at ten thousand feet tethered to a guy who I hoped knew what he was doing, I'd thrown myself all in with Sam and Dave and assumed they knew what they were doing. Now I briefly considered other scenarios. What if they forgot about me? Not likely. Suppose they got called away for any one of a hundred reasons. Maybe they just had enough of me and decided to let me waste away out here. Not a bad way to go. I could endure and enjoy this for as long as I could then unzip and be gone in a blink. That's what happens in the movies. I had no control over what may or may not happen in the upcoming minutes, so I opted for embrace. Enjoy. Trust.

The feeling of the vacuum of space is unlike anything I'd ever experienced. No resistance anywhere. I'd already accidentally slapped myself three times from lack of limb control. Too free. I held my arms and legs out from my body and took it all in. Stars. Millions of them. Time to ponder the immensity of the universe. Time to consider what had happened and what was about to happen. "Don't think meat, just react." (Catcher Kevin Costner to pitcher Tim Robbins in Bull Durham) And so, I relaxed and listened to the stars. This was better than any inversion table, hot tub, skydive, scuba dive or meditation I'd ever experienced.

I was hoping they wouldn't be back for a while. I put out of my mind that between me and the cold unforgiving vacuum was a thin layer of…. whatever it was. I wondered if I'd be allowed to keep the suit. I could see wearing this around the house. I let out an involuntary chuckle and the sound surprised me. I started a conversation with myself and the sound and sensation were weird. Vibratory. Enough. Back to groovin'.

The egg was back. How long had it been? Twenty minutes? It slowly came around and stopped about ten feet in front of me. For the first time I noticed how aerodynamically perfect the craft appeared. Dimly inside lit, it was striking in the blackness of the space around us. Maybe the fact that they returned, and I wouldn't float interminably through space for the next thousand years contributed to the beauty of the moment. How'd they possibly find me? What kind of intergalactic GPS were they using? Again, forgot to ask. They slowly approached me or maybe I approached them, but we collided, and I was through and inside guided by the sure alien hands of Sam and Dave. Long arms and hands but decidedly humanoid, I thought. I was glad to be back. They asked if I was comfortable in the suit. I said I was, and I suppose it was easier to leave it on me rather than control environments in different sections of the tiny egg.

I asked where we were. I thought it was time to get some information. I was going to have to answer a lot of questions. They seemed to perk up when I'd get curious. They both started to answer at once. Sam took charge. I started to feel that he was the senior guy here. He told me we were between, as it's known to us, the Alpha Centauri B system, part of a twin star system next in line to ours, and their home system. At this point I wasn't taking notes as I would later but memory and google seem to back this up. So, we were on our way to another star? I felt an affirmation. But I also felt it was up to me. How far was I willing to take this? I asked how long they'd been traveling the stars. They looked at each other and Dave thought to me," Since the enlightenment of about eight hundred years ago."

"What happened?" I said.

Dave said, "You wouldn't understand. It was an unusual time. You'll have your own enlightenment soon, everyone does. There's a shift in the familiar paradigm."

"Will we make it?" I asked. They both looked at me and I heard, in unison, "You've made it this far. "Again, that tiny grin. Then they went back to the iPad, conferred, pointed out, looked at each other, then me, and Sam said, "Do you want to continue?" I nodded. Another grin and I felt the egg power up.

I was gently pulled behind the ring. My hosts were already in their positions. It seemed I had my space, they each had their space and I could feel there were other spaces within this barrier going around the interior of the egg. How many I couldn't tell. There couldn't be many. They put down the pad and sat. They motioned for me to do the same. I trusted and sat. Something like a chair caught me. I was sitting in or maybe just being held by a force of some kind. It was comfortable and seemed to conform to me. I had a feeling we were in for a longer ride than what we'd had up to now. The elevator in the stomach feeling was here, the stars liquefied, and Sam and Dave seemed to be.... sleeping?

Part 3

**

1

Pressure in my bladder snapped me to. Sam and Dave appeared to be enjoying the ride, just a couple of cowboys out for a trail ride. The stars appeared solid, so we were at cruisin' speed. I'd been sleeping. The last thing I remember was they were sleeping. Who was driving? I caught their attention when I said, "I have to go to the bathroom."

Dave said nonchalantly, "Go ahead. It'll be fine." That cool British accent. It can convince you to do anything. Sometimes they would talk. Sometimes they'd telepathize. New word. I could no longer tell the difference. My helmet was off. My suit was still on. They had, I noticed, placed a small rectangular device on my chest that apparently kept me oxygenated. And the barrier was gone. Bare bones.

I relieved myself in the suit and I don't know where it went but it was gone. I gotta get one of these.

I asked," How long was I asleep?"

"You weren't actually asleep, but about two hours. This is still the void," Dave said. I had a feeling he used that word for my benefit, like he'd heard me think it and maybe felt it was as good a word as any. Empty space. I knew the Voyager spacecraft was out here somewhere. Another testament to humankind. It was hurtling through the void and still sending back information. Whoever eventually found it would be treated to Chuck Berry, works of art and other hints of where Voyager had come from. We come in peace. I felt a small letdown. We have to pick it up, man. C'mon enlightenment!

Where did one system end and the next one start? The space between the planets in our solar system felt comforting, like our sun had us all wrapped in a big furry blanket. No blanket out here. I wasn't looking at my fellow travelers, lbut I could tell the difference in their projected thought voices. Given our travels so far, I made a loose calculation that we were well out there. What's a light year or two when the power of the universe is your accelerator? As my feeble brain was pondering, I felt another light source way out there; tiny, small, larger, then quickly larger. Things moved rapidly out here. It was out to our left and almost simultaneously we were hovering outside what could only be, I hoped, the mother ship.

The size of the thing was enormous. The football field comparison doesn't do it. Small city? Small planet? There was a definite, fresh in my memory, Saturnian look to the craft. From a distance an amateur such as myself may have indeed thought that a small planet was being observed rather than a ship. It was a saucer. There was a slight bubble on top and a circular extension that projected downward from the middle of the saucer and had visible windows. The edge of the extension was about a third of the way in from the edge of the saucer and went all the way around. The drop-down section was four levels. I could see activity at each level through the windows. I wondered if my appearance would cause a ruckus or was this old hat for the inhabitants. The windows were large ovals, about ten to fifteen feet in diameter, exactly in the middle of each level and spaced twenty feet apart as if each room or space had its own window. I noticed that the extension was slowly rotating. The ship was a brilliant silver that almost seemed to appear and disappear at times. I don't think it actually did but the clean surface against the magnificent backdrop of space and the way my eyes interpreted it, well, I'd have to inquire. I didn't.

There were twenty or thirty eggs like ours hovering, as we were, or coming and going. I wondered if I was the only "guest" or were there other visitors from the earth or, given our proximity, from other worlds. Was this their way of introducing themselves? I suddenly felt small and unimportant. Up to now I thought this was all for my benefit. Maybe we were just an afterthought. I blurted out, "How many civilizations or planets with life are out there?" "How many stars in the sky?" came back to me. Ah, thank you, sensei. I was staring at the ship, but I'd recognized Sam's voice. I looked over and the fellas were focused on the iPad and a panel that had popped out of the wall. Visually, there was a lot to take in; mother ship, eggs bobbing and weaving and new technologies popping up in our own craft.

But I could see it. In roughly one hundred years we'd gone from the Wright Brothers on the beach at Kitty Hawk to walking on the moon and sending landers to Mars. We have crews on the international space station and unmanned crafts landing on asteroids. To again quote Mr Haldane, "Queerer than we CAN suppose." Could the signers of the Declaration of Independence have imagined computer chips, iPhones or even combustible engines? To suggest an electric light, let alone bits and bytes traveling through the air in microseconds, would have gotten one burned as a witch in 1600's Salem. Our advances seem to be increasing exponentially. Maybe that's what happens.

Maybe this is our enlightenment. More importantly there seems to be a humane enlightenment. It's dawning on us that we have to take care of each other, all the creatures and Mother Earth herself. "There but for the grace of God...."

There's the ugly side too, but we're waking up. Why else would I be taken on this adventure? If Sam and Dave's enlightenment had been going on for eight hundred years, and given our technological leaps in one hundred years, where will we be in five hundred, two thousand, ten or twelve thousand years. "Queerer than we can suppose." This all suddenly seemed more historic, important and less fun. Up to now I was a kid building a raft down in Greenbrook Park, a raft to be launched on the mighty...um ...Greenbrook Park Creek. The raft would usually sink after one of us stood on it but then it was on to the building of the wobbly go cart or the climbing of the mighty evergreen trees or careening down unknown trails on unsafe bicycles and on and on. Could I treat this as another adventure? The chance that this was a dream was still not out of the realm of possibility. But if not, I was not going to be able to translate all that had happened thus far in an intelligent and coherent manner to our science community. Again, maybe that's the idea, just a glimpse to the average guy. They could have picked an astrophysicist, but they didn't. They picked me. I don't ask too many questions; just watch, observe, try to take it all in and remember....... everything. I have to write this down, colors, smells, feelings.

" We'll be going inside in a few minutes, "Dave said as Sam handed me an iPad and instructed me to use my finger to write. There was a keyboard type device covered in weird hieroglyphics that faded as the face of the pad brightened. I drew a line, then another. I wiped back and they were gone. We're fast learners. I thought it best to keep things short. Ideas. Smells. Higgins Funeral Home. Flowers. Shapes. Egg. And so, the journal began.

Shortly we started moving in. We were farther away than I thought. The ship was massive! How big is big? We approached above the windowed, rotating portion and I noticed lines in the saucer section that could be doors or openings, entrances. We hung outside one and as it vanished, we proceeded to move in.

As we moved through, I could see that it hadn't vanished but had morphed into that gelatinous substance that was neither liquid nor solid. Or maybe it was liquid and solid depending on the situation. How about if what was passing through doors and walls became un-solid, slid through and reformed on the other side? That worked for George Reeves on one of the old Superman episodes. I forget the premise, but he learned to walk through walls. And this was a guy who all he had to do was put on glasses and everyone accepted him as Clark Kent. I didn't buy it then and now I think the work was being done on the side of the entrance, not what was entering. Either way, as my old English teacher used to say, "The thick plottens."

2

Would I be going home again? Or was this the type of thing that "Now that you've seen this, we'll have to kill ya?" I doubted that. Why else would I be brought here if not to spread the word. Hope for humanity. It gave me that feeling like you get in your belly when you remember vacation is coming up next week. We weren't alone. We had brothers, and, I assumed, sisters, out there willing to help and guide us through troubling times. They made it. We can too. What was the end game? Would we land on the White House lawn as I led Sam and Dave to our leader? Would they drop me off with a pat on the back and a hearty "Hi Ho Silver.... Away!" I had to start asking more questions. I was furiously taking notes but unlike people using their cell phone to take videos at concerts I was also trying to be in the moment. Notes would have to wait as we entered Mother Ship.

I expected to arrive into a flurry of hectic activity. Not so much. We were in a section of the saucer, a docking station. There were five rows from floor to ceiling circling the entire inside of this area. About every ten yards or so was a "station." Most had an egg. Some didn't. The eggs were sitting in a type of clamp and where someone would step out there was a walkway. The walkway went all the way around the interior and at several locations there were breaks that turned and apparently went deeper into the interior of the ship. Each level had a walkway and turnoffs. We continued across and docked at the top-level easing into a clamp and with no discernible thump or bump, stopped. The light inside our egg dimmed and the power seemed to die out. Like the egg, the interior of this part of the ship was comfortably lit in a kind of soft yellow.

It's hard to explain but it just felt good, mellow, healthy. The thought" Mellow Yellow" popped into my head along with Sopwith Camel. I caught a bemused look from Sam and an "I don't get it" look from Dave. Sorry. Random thoughts, pathways. The Acid Cat. The walls and ceiling were more of a dark white and in certain areas seemed to fade in and out at times. It reminded me of the camouflage blankets that soldiers were using to make them seem invisible. It kind of worked but you weren't quite sure exactly what you were or weren't seeing. They seemed to have the invisibility, surface melting thing down. The walkway went from the wall to about six feet out. It looked safe. The whole space was about the size of a large, really large, hotel lobby. I saw there was a window that went all the way around the edge of the ceiling providing a wonderful look at the universe. The bubble? I got that look of" Ready?" from Dave and we stepped onto the walkway.

3

I felt heavy. It was a struggle to keep up. Sam and Dave were a few steps ahead. Dave turned back to me and made an adjustment to the unit on my chest. Now I felt lighter than normal. Cool. The funeral home fragrance was present but not as strong as in the egg. I felt like I may have been getting the overflow from whatever they and the others on this ship were breathing. We turned into a long hallway that lit up in sections as we approached and dimmed and faded out as we were a few yards past. There was light enough to see ahead and behind, and it seemed to me that the increase and decrease of lighting could quickly get annoying. I kept that to myself.

The walls were concave with thin black lines in no discernible pattern. The curve was there but not enough to make it feel like a tunnel. It was a hall. It was like the egg with a flat floor and curved walls and ceiling that could apparently fade out at any time. Why that would happen here and there now and then I'd have to find out. I didn't. We were approaching a T. I was getting ready to turn left or right when a space the size of a large door appeared in the wall in front of us. Sam and Dave walked through, and I followed. What immediately struck me was the wall, or lack of wall, on the far side of the room. The room was circular and from the ceiling and almost to the floor and circumnavigating the room was a window. It was so clear that at first, I thought it opened into space. But I could see slight reflections. People. And they were all staring and grinning, that grin, at me. I scanned the room and there was a group of about seven or eight. I jumped as someone on my right touched me. A female. Curves, a slighter frame and softer appearance. Very human. Large eyes and short dark hair. The nose was the most obvious non-human feature but maybe not enough to elicit curious stares. And her tiny ears were hidden by slightly longer hair. She had, as they all had, a pale yellowish pallor.

Up to now I thought it had been the lighting, but they didn't look well, healthy. I would find out more about that. Her eyes were like those sixties' paintings of the girls with the large eyes and didn't look as unusual on her as they did on Sam and Dave. Were we related somewhere, somehow? They were all wearing the wet suit uniform except one guy who was wearing what looked like blue medical scrubs with slippers.

My new friend looked a little surprised at my surprised reaction but still gave me the old wrist grab. I was ready and a slight wide-eyed smile appeared on her face.

I said, "Hello."

She said," welcome, "and made a sweeping gesture of the room. She spoke out loud and it sounded somewhat muddy, like she'd practiced but didn't have it quite yet, and with a British accent. Had they been monitoring British TV or movies? Sam and Dave stepped back, and the entire group gave a resounding "Huzzah!" It wasn't exactly a huzzah but a shout of some kind that I hoped meant "Good to see you!" Or maybe it was a welcome back greeting to my traveling companions. I don't really like being the center of attention in any situation and I was beginning to feel like the newest addition to an intergalactic zoo. Uh oh. A quick flash of a particular Twilight Zone buzzed through my head.

There was a tilted table underneath the entire length of the window on the far wall. Several small monitors on a clean black surface made it look like a modern stove top. Some areas were lit, some were flashing, and some seemed to be rising and falling. We were standing on a walkway that went around each side of the room and ended with a two-step drop at each side of the table. Seats were attached to the table and seemed to be able to be pushed under and pulled out at three or four-foot intervals. The two that were out looked spartan and not at all comfortable but as I was finding out, looks could be deceiving. The room was only the size of a large living room, but it had the feeling of a nerve center. A domed ceiling lent a sense of gravity to the space. Without realizing it I was walking toward the window, descended the steps and stood in front of the large window. Even after my solo spacewalk this was impressive. Another star system. I suddenly felt far, far away from home.

I sat in one of the available chairs and as I'd come to expect, it was very comfortable. It molded to me but not in an oppressive way. Smart chairs? I was looking out at the scene in front of me, the blackness of space interrupted occasionally by the arrival or departure of an egg. I don't know if there was something being pumped through the ventilation system but with the soft lighting and laid-back aesthetic in this "nerve center" I was feeling very relaxed, content, a little dreamy and hungry. Man, I was hungry, and losing track of time. I was in my back yard about eight o' clock. We spent about forty-five minutes tooling around our solar system. I think they said an hour to get here. Had I jotted that down on the galactic iPad? Close to two and a half hours? I'd have to rethink the timeline with a clearer mind. And where was the iPad? It was past my bedtime.

I was rubbing my stomach as Dave handed me the pad and what looked like one of those erasers that we cleaned the blackboards with in grammar school. Ask and ye shall receive. "We must be in heaven, man!" I laughed as I realized this summer would be the fiftieth anniversary of Woodstock. A long time ago, in a galaxy...er...star system far, far away. Would I see another galaxy? Is that even possible? Sam, or maybe Dave had said not this time, I think. So, I guess they had. I looked up and a heavier set man, meaning a little less thin than Keith Richards, motioned me to eat. I took a bite. It was like a bland rice cake. Had I ever had a delicious mouthwatering, gotta have another, rice cake? No. But it was edible, and I ate the whole thing. I immediately felt better. Back in the game.

I sat back and took in the scene before me. For just a moment I forgot where I was. I could have been on a beach, or a mountain, or in my back yard enjoying the nighttime sky. It looked different. I'm no astronomer but I guess after sixty plus years of gazing up at the stars you get a sense of how things are supposed to look. You know or at least feel where the moon should be; the dippers, big and little, Venus, the North Star and the small star clusters. This looked different. It was unsettling. I thought, after the evening I've had, this was unsettling?

I looked to my left and blue scrubs was sitting a few seats away, toward the end of the table. He pulled off the hospital type head covering he was wearing and, cue the heavenly choir, he was human, or certainly appeared human. He was an older gentleman, seventies, with a light white mustache that I hadn't noticed and thick white hair. He was smiling. It was indeed a full human smile. I suppose at this point nothing should have surprised me, but this threw me for a loop. I started laughing and all I could say was, "How ya doin?"

He said, in perfect coiffed English," How'm I doin?"

"Are you here of your own volition," I said.

Volition? Where the hell did that come from? Too much Dragnet as a kid. I immediately felt embarrassed. Earthy. "Yes, he said. Yes, fifty-three years now." "It's wonderful to see and speak with someone from home."

"How?" I asked. He seemed a little giddy. I noticed that between the eraser cake and.... all this....my throat was very dry. Hefty Keith Richards handed me a plastic cup of what appeared to be, and indeed tasted like, water.

Blue scrubs said, "Like you. Offered a ride. Decided to stay. I'd graduated a year earlier as a medical doctor and this seemed too good to pass up. The education I've gotten and the people we've helped is immeasurable. They drop into the Earth system about every now and then for a close up look and were in the right place to be able to respond to your invitation." Did I just see a wink?

He continued," So I guess I could go back. But this is home now." He stopped. "You have a lot of questions."

I raised my eyebrows, "Ya think?"

He laughed and said, "You'll have to get your answers from them." He nodded toward Sam and Dave. I should have asked him their names while I had him there, but I didn't. He continued, "You're now the ambassador. I thought I originally would be but I'm not going back. You are." I hadn't really thought about that.

There were lots of logistics to consider. But not now. I just wanted to keep taking it all in. I looked up and the woman was there. Staring. She was pretty, cute. She looked like a young Sally Field. Gidget. I looked around and everyone was listening.

Doc said, "This is a home base of sorts, one of many. I can tell you that the idea, the mission statement, if you will, is to be better, to learn and one by one help other races to be better and learn. It's that simple. I have to go but I wanted to meet you. You are the chosen one," he said in mock seriousness as he opened his arms to the sky. "It was good to meet you." he said." But really, you're the messenger. I don't know how much help you'll be getting, if any, so good luck." And with that he got up and started to walk away.

"What's your name," I asked? He looked a little embarrassed and said, "Ben Franklin. Dr Ben Franklin." I said, "You've gotta be kidding!" He smiled. "Not THE Ben Franklin. Just the son of Mr. and Mrs. Joseph and Beatrice Franklin of San Angelo, Texas but it was always a good ice breaker." He swiped the brim of an imaginary fedora and walked up the two steps and through a door that I hadn't noticed. It was an actual sliding type door with a whooshy opening and closing sound. Why, I wondered? I forgot to ask. Well heck! That was interesting. Nice to meet ya, Doc.

Gidget pulled out a seat from under the table and sat down next to me. She pointed straight out and said, this time in a thought, "Gossamer." Like Sam and Dave her thought message came through as an idea, something I'd have to interpret. What did Gossamer mean? I knew what gossamer was, I think. But what was she trying to say to me? Out in front of us, how far I couldn't attempt a guess, was a large star, like our Polaris, but larger and brighter. There were three more stars as my eyes went to the right, decreasing in size and luminosity. Between each star were comets or asteroids or at least bright bodies of varying sizes moving between each. I assumed they were moving as most appeared to have visible tails. I had the feeling this was why they were here. I thought Gossamer was a feeling or maybe the name of this group, like our "Three Sisters." Gidget was nodding and smiling. Alright. Nailed it.

I jotted this scene down on the iPad that had somehow appeared in front of me. The page was full. I showed it to Gidget. She took my finger and placed it on a small area on the pad. The page minimized to the upper left. Really minimized. And a new page was born. Did we somehow get our iPad technology from them, 'cause this was definitely an iPad? I jotted a quick note, maximized the former page and looked back at my scrawls, phrases, thoughts and made a note to sort this out at some point while it's fresh. I really wanted to get it right and make sure I could interpret my scrawls.

I still do a Thursday morning radio show, twenty-eight years and counting. It's a mix of music, interviews, live performances, and tales from the wilds of New Jersey. I have three hours of freedom. During the week if I see or hear something interesting, I'll jot it down on whatever's handy. My show is free form, unplanned and many's the time I've opened up a "road note" only to find I have no idea what I saw, heard or was going to try to convey. More about that later. I'd have to do a better job of scrawling here.

Gidget said, "Enjoy your adventure. (my interpretation) Watch, learn and bring the message." I felt that was my cue to pack it up. Sam and Dave were standing behind me at the top of the steps. As I joined them, and we started walking Sam gently took the iPad. It shrunk to about the size of a postage stamp and he placed it in a small pouch on my sleeve. Like I said. That was no iPad. I followed Sam and Dave as they walked toward the door that was no door, the way we came in. I stopped briefly and looked around the room, at the group, whom I could feel were sending a lot of hope my way. I gazed out at the "Gossamer" and thought how much I'd seen and learned in the last fifteen or twenty minutes. How much more to come? And why me? Dr Benjamin Franklin I could see. But why me? And I guess the only answer was why not me? The door vanished and we walked through.

4

Even though Dr. Franklin's "You are the chosen one," was tongue in cheek, it kind of gave me the willies. I felt and feel that I just happened to be in the right place at the right time. Then I remembered what Dr. Ben had said, that they'd heard my invitation and were in the right place to drop in or something like that. When I'd stand out in my back yard at night with Molly, or by myself enjoying the night, I'd often throw out a "prayer" to the universe," If you're up there, come down." I never, in my wildest dream, thought anything would come of it. But there was a tiny part of me that thought if an extraterrestrial race was advanced enough to cross the immense vastness of space then maybe they were advanced enough to hear some shlub from NJ inviting them to the party. If this were just a serendipitous encounter (of the third kind) or a small part of a larger master plan, I'd have no way of knowing. Thinking of *Close Encounters of The Third Kind*, maybe I was Richard Dreyfuss. The ET's passed on the scientists, intellectuals and anyone who thought they should be the "chosen one." and snatched up Richard to go for the ride. Why? That never really gets answered. They saw something.

We were approaching the loading dock area, but we turned left down an open corridor and about twenty feet further stepped into a depression on the right wall. It was large enough to hold four or five people and immediately got very bright when we stepped in. Dave waved at or touched something on the wall and the hallway in front of us disappeared, melted away. A few seconds later a different hallway materialized in front of us. It was wide, maybe ten feet and led straight out, a long way out. I don't know if the "elevator" moved or we transported or how the heck we got here but here we were. I'd have to ask. I didn't, but made a note in my iJournal. Sam dropped back, put his hand on my shoulder and asked how I was feeling.

"Slightly overwhelmed," I said. Dave looked back, gave me a grin and vanished to the left. Sam pointed to a vague imprint of a door on our immediate right and said, "I'll be in here." He walked me a few feet further to the next imprint and said, "We need to rest now. You should, too. "In and out, "he said and placed his hand over a small, raised area. A door whooshed open. Weird. Some whooshed, some disappeared, and some melted away. We walked in.

Cool. My own interstellar room. There was an obvious bed, a desk that had a kidney shaped pool look to it and another room which I correctly, as it turned out, assumed to be a bathroom. I guess some things are universal. There was an oval window, a porthole, like you would see on a boat. It was tiny but as Sam approached the wall it expanded. He walked back and it retracted. He showed me a series of patches on the wall across from the bed. Along that wall was a small couch and a chair divided by a table with a plant of some kind on it. Very Holiday Inn. Dave held his hand over one of the patches and the lights dimmed and then brightened. He held his hand over another one and a picture/video of a room like mine appeared.

"That's my room," Dave said. "Just speak." Again, I'm translating but that was the jist. He pointed to the bathroom which he seemed to know I understood. He walked across the room and as he stood in front of the wall just past the bottom of the bed a concave space (closet?) opened. There were two "wetsuits," a cool black bathrobe and feet attire, slipper type things with separate toe areas like we see these days on earth. Unfortunately, there was only space for four toes. Ah, evolution.

Sam handed me another "rice cake" and said, "You'll figure it out. You're free to wander but please stay here for now. Rest. Eat. Sleep. We'll meet later. Lots to show you."

"You've been a great host," I said. "Thank you"

"This is the best part of my job," he said. Interpretation. And with that he turned, the door whooshed and I was alone.

I lost track of time. I figured it was well past my bedtime, maybe somewhere around midnight. Could I possibly fall asleep? What was Linda doing, besides freakin' out. And who could blame her. I guess I could have demanded to be brought home, but I couldn't. This was starting to feel important. She'd understand. But still, I felt bad leaving her with this. Would she tell anyone? Keep it to herself? For all she knew I wouldn't be coming back. For all I knew I wouldn't be coming back. Raised on Twilight Zone, Outer Limits and assorted science fiction books and movies involving ……. this……., I assumed anything was possible. I'm a pretty good people reader and all I was getting were good vibes from everyone. If I didn't get back how would she explain this?" No, really, he entered an egg like craft with an alien and they took off into the nighttime sky. That's the last time I saw him. Honest!" (You have the right to remain silent, ma'am.) I'd have to ask if there was any way to contact her.

I went to the closet, slipped into the bathrobe which seemed to adjust itself it to me, passed on the four toed slippers, hung up the wetsuit then lay down on the bed. The bed eased up into a pillow at the top and I felt a perfect warmth from head to toe, like I was in a blanket but there wasn't any. How'd they do that? That was becoming my mantra. I closed my eyes and that's the last thing I remember.

5

Invaders from Mars, The Thing, Destination Moon, The Day the Earth Stood Still, War of The Worlds, Star Wars. And, of course, the world of television with the various Star Treks, Outer Limits, Twilight Zones and The Million Dollar Movie which featured movies of all kinds five nights a week and twice on Saturday and Sunday. My head was filled with a hundred different scenarios as I woke up into that dreamy half sleep. Morning, night, early afternoon, I didn't know but I don't remember ever being this comfortable. (Ma, I don't wanna get up!) I immediately knew where I was. I felt rested and clear. As I lay there, I decided, again, to just be all in, go with the flow. I wasn't completely sure if I had a choice or not, but that moment would come at some point.

I threw my feet over the side of the bed and went to the closet to retrieve the iPad. The floor was warm on my bare feet. I go barefoot whenever possible. I approached the faint outline of the closet and sure enough it opened and was softly illuminated. I took the iPad out of the sleeve of yesterday's wetsuit and sat on the couch. Before I got too comfortable that familiar morning pressure led me to the bathroom. It was a small room to the left of the kidney desk which lit as I walked in. There was a toilet and a sink; a wildly futuristic looking toilet and sink but a toilet and sink, nonetheless. I did my thing, heard a soft whoosh (whoosh seemed to be a popular sound around here) and it was ready for the next guy. An area which may or may not have been a shower took up most of the other wall. There was no visible shower head, but I had a feeling that if I stepped over there something would happen. I walked to the sink and put my hands under a faucet looking device that came up and out of a shallow sink. Immediately a wide stream of dry water shot out. It was really more like a gas. I kept my hands there and I didn't want to take them out. It felt great! A very odd sensation. I assumed if there was anything here that could harm me someone would have mentioned it. I didn't see a towel of any kind but as my hands weren't wet it didn't matter.

I went back to the couch. Could I get a cup of coffee? Room Service! The monitor above my head came to life and there was Gidget. (Surf's up!)

She said, "Hello. I hope you slept well. Is there anything you'd like?" I didn't want to seem pushy, but I was hungry. The rice cake was sitting on the other desk, but I thought I'd take a shot.

"I'd love some cereal with milk and a cut up banana, a glass of orange juice and a cup of coffee," I said making sure she noticed my ironic smile.

She said, "Wait thirty seconds then press the button next to the plant on your desk, the white one." As I was looking for the white button Gidget gave a small wave and the screen blipped off. Who was in charge of me? What was the hierarchy? Don't think, meat, just react. I realized I was sitting there in a bathrobe and didn't know how appropriate that was, so I opted for another wetsuit. I pulled a black one out of the closet, stepped into it and it sealed itself onto me. Boy, this makes getting dressed in the morning so much easier. I hung the bathrobe up. I wanted to be a good guest. There was no bed to make.

I walked back to the couch and stared at the white button. I pressed. What happened next was profound. On a small depression next to the white button appeared my breakfast, cereal with milk and a cut up banana, orange juice and a cup of black coffee. It materialized out of nowhere! I gotta get one of these, too. I usually like a little milk in my coffee, but this would do. I wondered if I could do that myself. I thought I probably could and like Sam said, I'd figure it out. There was a metallic spoon on a cloth napkin next to a beautiful peacock blue bowl of cereal. Did I say Holiday Inn? No disrespect but this was Hilton. I tried the cereal and it was very tasty. Kind of Wheaties meets Frosted Flakes. The milk was cold and hit the spot. The OJ was OJ, banana was banana and the coffee was coffee. I thought this may have the hand of Benjamin Franklin on it. He had to eat, didn't he? Thanks Doc. A magical meal. There are certain meals that stand out, that rise above and beyond the superb, even outstanding dining experience that is not always a result of the food but the experience that accompanies the food. This was one. There was another.

On my first trip to Yankee Stadium, circa '62 - '63, my father and I stepped off the bus at the New York Port Authority and walked the two blocks to the Horn and Hardart Automat before boarding the Subway uptown. The Automat was a New York staple and an eye opener for a ten-year-old kid from Plainfield. There was anything you wanted behind little glass doors. Put in a dime, quarter, whatever it demanded, lift the glass door and voila. Lunch. I pulled out a baloney sandwich and somehow it was one of the best baloney sandwiches I ever had. My dad said why don't I go get a piece of cherry pie. He knew, everyone knew, that a piece of cherry pie did not stand a chance on a plate in front of me. Alright. I'll bite. I took my dime, surveyed the dessert area and…. Xanadu! There were four or five glass doors that held back picture-perfect slices of cherry pie, apple pie and the much-maligned blueberry pie. I snatched one before anyone found out about this gastronomic miracle and hightailed it back to our table overlooking forty fourth street and succumbed to the gustatory sensation of the pie in all its cherry goodness. I was without speech.

The only thing that could possibly come close to equaling the majesty of this lunch would be watching the New York Yankees beat up on the Cleveland Indians, complete with a bench clearing brawl led by the always unpredictable Jimmy Piersll. (Check out "Fear Strikes Out" with Tony Perkins and Karl Malden.) That was a day that would live in infamy.

I finished up my first interstellar meal and left it where I found it. I walked over to the other desk and the oval window started to expand. I tried to expand it like on an earthly laptop, with my fingers. That didn't work. It was open to the size of a typical big screen tv and that was good enough. I put the postage stamp size iPad on the desk in front of me and tried the laptop expansion again. It expanded to its original size and stopped. Alright! I had to get this down. It was all too much. Maybe just a detailed outline would do. I didn't know how much time I'd have so I got to it.

6

I had no idea what the itinerary was for the day, or night, or whenever this was so I spent the next twenty minutes or so jotting, remembering, star gazing and waiting for the call to action. I covered three pages on the interstellar iPad when Sam's face popped up on the window. As I looked a little closer, I saw his face wasn't on the window, it was hanging in the air, kind of like the dashboard hologram that cars had or may still have. Like a lot of new technology, it's cool for a while then…. why? But c'mon man, how'd he do that? He asked if I'd like to look around The Home.

That was a direct translation, The Home. That had a bit of a creep factor to it. Kind of cultish. Trust, my brother, trust. Did they live here or was it like our space station, extended duty and done? Were they FROM here? Is that what happens? Life in space? No home planet? When I asked where they were from Sam, or Dave, pointed to an area out there. I thought he said three stars from us. Two? Got to look into that.

I said I'm ready anytime and Sam shrunk and popped out of sight. It actually made a pop. Once again, too cool. There was a knock on the door. A knock!! I expected better.

"C'mon in," I said, and Dr Ben and Gidget whooshed into my room followed by good morning's all around. I guess it was morning somewhere. That was probably for my benefit.

Benjamin Franklin was wearing his blue scrubs but on closer inspection it looked more like a sweat suit, comfortable and lots of jiggle room, and sneakers! Gidget was wearing the same wetsuit as yesterday, a few hours ago, last week? I was lost in a time warp. Gidget went over to my breakfast "dishes," bing, bang, boom and they were gone. I'd have to find out how to do that. I'm no Felix Unger but I like to clean up my own mess, especially when I'm a guest in someone else's home. Dr Ben was checking out my iPad and said, "Can you actually read that?" I liked him. He was one of those people that I immediately felt comfortable with. Why does that happen. Chemistry? Because he was like me? Everyone I've met so far has made me feel very much at ease. Was that something they were doing to me? Was it in the air? Ahhh, so many questions, grasshopper. My writing looked like a cross between type and script, I think.

I said, "I'm gonna have to do a lot of editing, but as I looked at it, no. I can't really read it. "I started laughing. He started laughing. We were both hysterical and he was wiping his eyes.

"Been a long time," he said. It felt good. I've seen a lot of smiles, wry and otherwise but no guffaws. It did feel good. Gidget was looking and smiling. Ben said, "Wanna go for a walk?" I gave a nod and turned off the iPad. I'd noticed a wave of the hand did it, and stood, taking a last glance out the window.

7

About twenty years ago I took a trip to the Cayman Islands. My future ex-wife didn't want to take time off from work, so she gave me her blessing and off I went. I enjoy doing things on my own now and then. I think we need it. Oh, to be left alone with your deepest thoughts and fears. Last summer I went to a local reservoir, kayaked a few miles out to the campsites and did an overnight adventure. I still have a scar on my left hand where I tripped into the fire ring in the middle of the night. It's dark out there, man. An adventure, of any kind, is good for the soul. The adventures get safer as I get older, but they still feel like adventures. Maybe more so.

There's something cool, fun about going where you want to go when you want to go. A few years pre-Cayman Islands and pre marriage I took a two-month cross country sabbatical. Great word, sabbatical. Fresh credit card, new tires and I was off. I stopped at my old school in El Paso for a day, visited my nephew in Arizona and wound up in San Diego. There seemed to be a set of "eyes" following me on that venture. My brakes finally gave out in La Jolla. I pulled into one of those funky little seaside hotels, looked in my rear-view mirror and saw the words "Brake World." Actually, I saw, "dlroW ekarB." Thanks universe. I took the Pacific Coast Highway to San

Francisco stopping at the Hearst Castle, the canyons of LA (I'd spent an Easter break in a mansion in Laurel Canyon in 1971. Another time), spent a psychedelic couple of hours in La Honda listening to a guitar player at a cool little outside bar and scoping out the Ken Kesey Prankster house across the way. I hung outside the old Grateful Dead home in Frisco and managed to get a room in Carmel during the busiest time of year involving some kind of car race. I enjoyed a small earthquake on the beach at Morro Bay then cut across to Las Vegas for a few days of glitz and glamour. Vegas has a similar feeling to my current astronomical residence in that there is no sense of time. I went to the Grand Canyon with my future ex-wife, Donna, who flew out for a short stint, then I drove back solo with a brief stop at Meteor Crater, a large impact crater in northern Arizona. It was only two hundred and fifty miles out of the way. After working my way through the Meteor Crater gift shop, there it was. The moon! Or a close facsimile. Then home to New Jersey.

I share this only to show that I don't mind being alone. Be it throwing a ball off the steps of a porch on W. Sixth St, wandering around Meteor Crater or waiting for a brake job in San Diego, I've always been good at entertaining myself. There's nothing like sharing a sunset, a baseball game, dinner, concert or movie with someone you love but alone time is good, too. It's healthy, I think.

I got caught up staring into the black void with Dr Benjamin Franklin and Gidget. The depth and emptiness of the scene before me and only a few feet away was spookily reminiscent of the long-ago solo trip to Grand Cayman. With no one to suggest where to go or what to do I joined a small group for a submarine adventure off the coast and near the tip of the Cayman Trench. Rumor on the sub was that this was where the movie The Abyss was filmed but I couldn't verify that. The small sub was cruising the blue waters off Grand Cayman when the lights went out and we drifted out and over something, nothing. We were hovering over the 22,000-foot-deep Cayman Trench. The lights of the sub were trained downward but all we could see was blue, darker blue, darker blue then finally, black. It felt desperately lonely and a little unsettling. I sensed a slight vertigo. The captain dropped us a bit and a few shrieks escaped the group. I don't think I shrieked but I can't be sure. We went out a little further then came back in. Stepping onto the dock felt good.

Now I was staring into the "Abyss" with Gidget and Ben. Familiar. I looked at Dr. Franklin and he was staring, too. "I never get tired of that," he said.

"Remember it," I said, as I thought of Horseshoe Bay and the stunningly blue water of Bermuda.

I chirped, "Lead on, McDuff!" That elicited another cackle from Ben and a quizzical smile from Gidget. Off we go then.

8

We exited my room. We didn't head back the way I'd come in but continued along the hall. This was obviously a housing area as doors ran all the way along both sides of the corridor with similar symbols (numbers?) on each. I remembered Sam was a few doors down from me. Would he be looking for me? We exchanged casual greetings with people we passed, some staring, others just smiling, all decked out in the cool wetsuits with the exotic symbol on the upper right. I wondered about the significance of the logo if it was a designation of rank or maybe a name tag. After a few turns we stopped at what I now recognized as the "elevator." The three of us got in as the far wall evaporated, and a large open space shortly appeared in front of us. This, I felt, was the top of the ship, saucer. It was a large space with numerous tables, chairs, couches and leaning type devices. The leaners looked like large wicker baskets designed to conform to the body that leaned back so the inhabitant could look up and around. Some were filled. Many were vacant. A few had a small desk type contraption that came up and out. It could be expanded depending on its use at the moment. I assumed that as the desktops were different sizes. Some people were working, some socializing in different size groups and some were just wicker basket groovin'. A window started about halfway up the wall and continued all the way up and around. Viewed from the outside and directly above, this would look like a transparent dime, where we were, sitting on a quarter, sitting on a half dollar. The rest of the ship continued out in all directions from there. I'd get the outside view a little later. This space was about the size of a large gym but quiet, softly lit and comfortable.

Rutgers college had, or used to have, a small building called The Ledge. It was a combination cafeteria, hang out, coffee house and would have small concerts every now and then. Rutgers was only a few miles from our neighborhood, and it was an interesting place to hang out. I saw Bruce Springsteen and the E Street Band there in 70' or 71', before "Greetings from Asbury Park." My pal Finny and I had gone to the Ledge to see a local blues band and when they were done Bruce and the boys came on. They weren't advertised and just looked like a bunch of guys in surfer shirts hanging around backstage. The place was only about half full and people were starting to roll out when the E Street Band kicked in. Like an old rock and roll movie people started turning around and slowly walking back toward the stage. Bruce started out slow and wound up rockin' the joint. We were standing in front of the slightly elevated stage and about three feet from the boss. I never saw anyone connect with a crowd like that. He was different. That was the only time I ever saw the E Streeters but they left an impression.

The area of the ship we were in had a feeling of Ledge meets Student Union meets library meets pub. People looked up every now and then, but I guess they'd observed many races from many places and seemed polite but mainly disinterested. I wanted to find someone and chat. At both ends of the room were what looked like bars. I thought I'd be bold, walk to the closest bar on our left, sidle up and ask for a beer. There was an outline of a person behind the bar in a few different spots. I thought I'd take a shot. I said to the faux bartender, "I'd like a beer please." As in my room a beer shimmered to life.

I said to Ben who appeared next to me, "Is this safe?" He nodded. I drank. It was, indeed, beer. Ben ordered something I didn't recognize and motioned to an empty table. Gidget had disappeared. Time for some answers.

9

"Aldair (All - Dare) is where these fine people come from. And they are fine people." Dr Ben continued. "I'm not sure why they picked you as I'm not sure why they picked me, but we can only hope to become half what they've become. They don't judge and they don't give a lot of answers. Clues, hints, helpful shortcuts. Watch and listen." He slowly surveyed the room.

"I hate to sound, well, racist, I said, but they all seem to look very much alike and not well."

He laughed, "And we all look alike to them."

I said, "Why Aldair."

The good Dr. replied, "Why Earth?" Touche'.

He went on to tell me that part of their message relates to that, their look and demeanor. Like the Earth, Aldair had separate indigenous races, seven in all. They went through their growing pains but eventually coexisted peacefully, married, or something equivalent, and had children. After many thousands of years their emotions had been bred out of them and they became physically weak and more easily susceptible to disease.

They instituted strict rules about having children outside their respective races but relationships among races were still acceptable. He didn't get into any accompanying penalties, if any. As a result, their emotions have started to return and physically they've become stronger. It's taken generations but it's worked. He told me they no longer fall in love but choose compatible mates to further their population, although some "stirrings are starting to arise." I had to think about that.

I said, "We're human. We have emotions. Strong emotions. I can deliver the message, but I wouldn't expect much. You weren't far removed from World War Two and a guy who talked about racial purity. That message won't sit well with just about anyone."

"Again, Ben said, they're not talking about separation. Fall in love. Get married. Don't procreate outside your race." I know they were just looking out for us but that made a chill go up my back.

"Just to let you know, he said, they don't expect you to take their advice. No one does. They were at a point where they had to take drastic measures and it worked for them so far. You have time. And that, he said is the message. One part of the message."

He continued," They may also help you overcome medical stumbling blocks by giving you information that you can expand on leading to eradication of disease. They also may not. I'm not sure why."

"All disease?" I asked.

He replied, "All disease."

I inquired, "When do they die? Do they die?"

"All things die. He said, plants, animals, planets, star systems you, me, them. The quality of a healthy life is everything and they know when it's over." I had lots of questions.

As we finished up our drinks, and that was a really good beer, he told me they'd like to show me Aldair. That got my attention. But first I had to try out one of those cool wicker recliners.

10

As I was "wickering" a few Aldairans stopped by to welcome me and ask a few simple questions. Why do we still kill each other? Um......I don't know. Why are we so distant from each other? Well, that's getting better. Why do we mistreat our planet? Also, getting better. Why isn't our scientific community more invested in interstellar travel or at least going out and finding future homes as Earth will not be able to support the coming population? I have thought about that. I figured by the time we ran out of room we'd have a plan in place. Sooner or later, we will have to leave. I got thoughtful, non-emotional nods to my responses. Polite but reserved. No judgment, just curiosity. I left it with, we're getting it, it's slow and we're trying. I liked these guy and ladies. Two women were part of the friendly inquisitors, longer hair and curvier bodies than the men.

Dave stopped by and asked if he could escort me back to my room. I don't know if it was the beer, the inquiries or just the emotional intensity of this experience but I suddenly felt weary. I was on a flying saucer with an alien civilization light years from Earth! I needed a nap. On the way back to my quarters Dave bounced the idea of a trip to Aldair off me. I was curious how much time this would involve even though whatever his answer was I'd have to sign on. He assured me I'd be home in a few days, but they wouldn't be making themselves known to us until a few days after that. And that was still under discussion. I didn't quite get it, but I was on board.

Back in my room I got to note taking. Fast and furious and hopefully, legibly. Later I managed to order a grilled cheese sandwich on whole wheat and a cold glass of water from the wavy food machine. I forgot to ask Dr Ben about his influence or lack of influence on the quality of the earthly food. Either way, compliments to the chef. I lay down on the space bed and was out.

Part 4

**

1

Sam, Dave and I were back in the egg hurtling through the universe once again. We humans are nothing if not adaptable. This was starting to feel normal, comfortable. We'd been out about forty-five minutes. I knew that meant we were covering some ground, some space. We'd left the "Mother Ship" with no fanfare. I kind of thought I would have created more of a stir. You know that feeling when you tell everyone not to make a big deal out of your birthday, then they don't? Like that.

Sam was seated and seemed transfixed by the space whizzing by us. The stars were watery, so I knew we were in overdrive. I'm not sure where the "Mother Ship" was, besides the "void," and never thought to ask. They had said their home was two stars to the right of our sun. Now, at this speed we must be…. I do not know. My head hurt. But I was copiously note taking. It seemed perfectly credible that they could travel intergalactically. Had they mapped the entire universe. I looked up at Sam and heard, "Not possible. (smile) It's growing faster than we can keep up." He went on, "We have a vessel, like the one we just left, on its way to what you call Andromeda. It will be a multi-generational trip and our second step outside your and our galaxy. They have been out for thirty-seven years and are currently beyond, and well into the intergalactic void. If I gave the impression that we had traveled to other galaxies I apologize. This is the second Aldairan group to undertake such a mission. They're explorers. What they will find or when and if we'll ever hear from them again is unknown. We never heard from the first group but the trajectories are the same. We're hoping they can find each other. The earlier communication signal is gone, and the second communication signal is progressively weakening." A palpable feeling of sadness mixed with pride descended on the egg. I wondered if they had friends or family members on one or both of those missions.

I can't describe it, but I felt warmer, not physically but...spiritually? The emptiness of the void was gone.

"Your neighbor, I heard. Alpha Centauri." Ah, the next blanket. I thought this may be the twin star system. I knew just enough to get myself in trouble. I appreciated the Anglicization of terms and landmarks for my benefit.

"Life? "I asked.

No response but Sam got up to confer with Dave and then the stars became once again solid. A red and blue ball came into view

"Your home?" I asked.

"No, Sam said. "A developing civilization much like yours centuries ago. We thought you may find it interesting. Then on to Aldair if you'd like." My head was ready to explode. Why was I given this tremendous opportunity? I thought there could still be a chance I was dreaming. Everything seemed so surreal yet natural. Why?

The egg suddenly seemed very fragile to me. So many "what ifs" popped into my head. After my "walk." the vacuum of space was very real to me. Space was empty. I mean nothing. The absence of anything. Except cold. My ninth-grade science teacher used to say that cold is a lack of heat, but heat is not a lack of cold. We were surrounded by an overwhelming and unforgiving lack of heat. Trust, Lyons, trust.

Dave gave me that look that said, "Ready?" Something interesting always followed that. I gave a wave of the hand towards the hovering ball and down we went, slowly. As opposed to the way they approached my backyard this was a Sunday drive. Land masses, two large ones, were becoming clear as were two large bodies of water. We were circling the planet slowly. If you've ever watched the Nasa channel, much like the Yule Log at Christmas, Earth View is just that, an extended shot of Earth from, I assume, the International Space Station. I always found it interesting to watch for a few minutes. So spoiled. What would the historical Benjamin Franklin say if someone asked him if he'd like to watch a real time view of the Earth from space?

The thin atmosphere of the egg between us and the void seemed so tenuous. I had my suit with the small pad on the front providing, I guessed, everything I needed. Sam and Dave were sans helmets. What were they breathing, I wondered? How long would I last without my magic button?

"Oxygen, I heard, like you. But of a much thinner composition. You could survive for some hours, but you wouldn't feel well and would eventually succumb. The "button" enhances the atmosphere for you. "The planet below appeared around the size of Earth from the Nasa "Earth Views. "On each go around, we got closer. There were two large land masses, one being extremely mountainous. And the two bodies of water really seemed to be one large ocean. I guess Earth's oceans could be seen as one large ocean but here the two gigantic land masses emphasized that.

It was about the size of the Earth by my feeble calculations. Sam and Dave had their heads together over the iPad. I got up and walked to the wall of the egg. I'm not sure why the barrier that held the seats was there if I could walk through it. I'd have to ask. I didn't but did make a note. I looked over at my fellow travelers and they were looking at me. I realized I had both palms up on the wall of the egg. They seemed to enjoy the tour they were giving me.

As a limo driver there was nothing I liked better than taking someone to New York for the first time. I'd pop the roof vent and there it was. Tall! And I always told them to look up. Some of the best stuff is up. Gargoyles hanging onto the sides of buildings, great old architecture, rooftop bars and gardens etc. If I or they had time I'd always try to show them something. Maybe a spin through Central Park or Greenwich Village. And as the guide I could say pretty much whatever I wanted. Depending on where they were from would dictate the parameters of my content. "Oh, you're from Shanghai? First time? Well to our left is Macy's, the pride of thirty fourth St, designed in nineteen seventy-nine by the late Bill Macy, who coincidentally made a mark as Walter, the husband and foil to Bea Arthur's TV character Maude." And so on. Some things, of course, were right on. I could amaze my passengers by explaining that the acronym of Dumbo stood for down under the Manhattan Bridge Overpass. "Oooohs" from the back seat. Sam and Dave didn't need to pad or inflate anything. I wondered if they did, anyway.

2

We were close now. Cloud layers were streaming past and I was getting sight of cuts in the ground that could only be roads.

"Won't they see us?" I asked.

Dave said, "Maybe, but probably not. It doesn't matter. We haven't contacted this race yet." So much for the Prime Directive, I thought. I wondered if we could somehow get shot out of the sky by a hostile civilization. A barrier appeared outside the egg. A field of some kind that surrounded us for about fifteen feet out on all sides. I looked over at Sam. He touched something and the field disappeared.

He said, "It's always there. Feel better?" Was that humor? I could no longer tell when they were thinking to me or talking to me. I'd also very quickly got used to the intermittent eye blinks. They all had it. Again, we are adaptable creatures.

We were cruising over a large, beautiful azure body of water. I couldn't see land anywhere. We were skimming about twenty-five feet off the water at a speed, I'd guess, of about sixty to seventy miles per hour. Man, this was cool! Sam and Dave looked like they were just having fun. Dave pointed down to the left and we were shortly flying alongside what looked like our idea of Noah's Ark. It was huge, appeared wooden with no sails or visible people, but was moving along by some means of propulsion.

I saw a large school of fish, or aquatic life form, keeping up with the ark on all sides. They were about the size of tuna and stayed, at least while we were there, submerged. They moved in and out from the sides of the vessel in unison, like schools of earthly fish, or those huge flocks of birds that seem to know where and when to go. Then they stop looking like birds and take on the appearance of some strange gracefully gyrating pattern. The fish I was seeing reminded me of those earth critters. They looked like a breathing mass that was an extension of the ark. It almost looked like the ark was getting pulled through the water by the fish like creatures. Was it? (no answer) The ark was an impressive dark brown and the wide slats of wood or some distant cousin to wood, gave it a majesty as it slid through the four to five-foot waves. The ark was about three times the size of the large "rich and famous "yachts of Earth. I was curious as to who or what was inside and how the ark was moving. Again, no answer.

We pulled up and out and increased speed dramatically. The color of the water lightened to a stunning clarity and a shoreline was becoming visible along with distinctive groups of large red coral. I've never been on a helicopter, but this had to be close to that experience. We were screaming along about two hundred feet above the surface and were quickly approaching a beach area. We continued inland then up and over a forest or jungle that suddenly appeared. The egg slowed and slowed then came to a hover over a clearing below. It was a village, a small town. No, it was a village. We came to rest a few feet off the ground just outside the perimeter or what I took to be the perimeter of the village. There was activity. People, beings were moving around. My heart was about to pop out of my chest. Dave touched my arm. "Don't worry. he said. They can't see us." A picture popped into my head of the invisibility blankets that our military had been working on. I looked at Dave and he made a motion that we were within such a blanket. "Sometimes we can be sensed," he said.

Beings were walking within fifteen or twenty feet of us. They were short, maybe four feet tall and the best description is their heads were large and strangely resembled the Easter Island statues. Slits for eyes, huge noses and large lips over a long square chin. A rough, gray complexion gave them an actual stone like appearance. Very off putting. They resembled participants in a New Orleans parade where large masks are worn covering the head and half the torso. The arms and legs were symmetrical to the torso and as they were naked male and female were easily recognizable. Dwellings, of which I could see about twelve or fifteen, were constructed of piled up rocks with smoke coming out of a few visible chimneys. What seemed to be a female child walked toward us. She stopped about three feet away and stared. Time to go. Reverse, then straight up. The child's eyes were following us. I guess we were "sensed."

Then something very odd happened. The child removed her head, only to reveal, her head! They were wearing large masks. Wow. Note to self. Do not take anything at face value. A beautiful face of a child was revealed, more human looking than the Aldairans, with bronze coloring and straight jet-black hair. She could have been a cousin to our early native Americans. Except for the short stature they were us. I wondered if the human form was a constant or will we eventually run into the huge bug like creatures of the 1950's movies. I wondered but didn't ask. I felt like I'd just seen an ancient Mayan village. A brief feeling of euphoria came over me. Why or from where I don't know. But a weird comfortable peace washed over me.

We are not alone. And as much as we like to think we are, we aren't that special.

We were cruising about three hundred feet over the forest canopy. It was huge and the tops of the trees were a beautiful Autumn leaves type red. I'd guess every seventy-five miles or so a hole would open up in the canopy and a small town similar to the one we'd left would appear. We passed eight or nine of these, some larger and some smaller. We didn't descend again. Sam looked at me with that "That's somethin' to tell the folks back home, eh," grin. Yes indeed, Sam. Yes indeed.

3

The planet was shrinking below us and shortly we were back out in the cosmos to resume out trip to...where? I was overloaded with questions but was trying to stick to my just let it all wash over me tack. Maybe I was being lazy because asking all the questions and trying to decipher, understand and remember all the answers would really take a lot of work and focus.

I once took a guitar lesson from renowned New Jersey jazz guitarist Harry Leahey. He is no longer with us but, man, he could play. I left that half hour lesson with a ream of lessons, notes, scales, exercises etc. Harry said when you get that down, come back. I wasn't that serious a guitar player, so I'd sit down with the Harry lessons every few weeks. They were well laid out and if I took the time it all made a lot of sense. During the lesson I listened and observed but mostly let it all wash over me, to be sorted out later. I was in that mode now; throw a load of info at me, see what sticks and sort it out later. I assumed we and the Aldairans were now connected and eventually they'd be sharing notes with our scientific community and whomever else may be interested. I could give an overview, bullet points, but Sam and Dave and the gang would have to sharpen the points. At least that was my hope.

I wasn't directed to the "safe" area behind the barrier so I assumed we wouldn't be traveling long. Dave touched an area on the wall/window and a screen opened up. With his finger he directed it to the area in front of him. Like earlier, it seemed frozen in space. He could move it wherever he wanted, and it would stay put.

I'd been wearing the interplanetary spacesuit which was starting to feel very comfortable. The attached shoes part was like walking on clouds and adjusted to my wide feet and five toes perfectly. The subject of their toes, four or five, never came up. I had the air exchange apparatus on my chest but now Sam asked me to put a helmet on. I didn't ask questions. He handed me the helmet, I placed it over my head, and it slid and snapped into place inside the top of my suit. I looked around and the planet had disappeared. "You might want to sit," Dave said. I went to the area behind the barrier and the chair was waiting for me. I sat down and I was out. I don't know how they did that and, of course, didn't ask. Maybe they just wanted to keep me out of the way. I thought I'd been a perfect guest, not too yappy, not too many questions, but expressing the correct amount of awe and excitement. I was really trying to be cool, staying out of the way but being involved when appropriate. I reminded myself just how huge this was. First contact. At least the first contact that would be an Earth event. I hoped. And it was me. I'd be leaving the heavy lifting to the experts back home. I just wanted to soak up impressions.

I had a chance to get backstage at a Grateful Dead concert in the mid-seventies. The show was at Roosevelt Stadium in Jersey City, NJ. The stadium was a minor league baseball park that doubled as a concert venue, not too big, not too small. The first shot at the show had gotten rained out and the Dead returned about five days later, Jerry Garcia's thirtieth birthday. I was with three pals and we wound up down in front of the stage. I'd seen the Dead two or three times prior and besides the music, the carnival atmosphere was always entertaining. I was never a fan of the spacey type jams they'd get into but on this Jersey City summer night they rocked from beginning to end. I ran into another friend who handed a birthday cake up to Jerry. He seemed happy to receive it. But Captain Trips (a name Jerry was not fond of) always seemed happy. At a GD concert there was always the chance you might get separated from the group and wind up on your own adventure. If you could make it back to the car all was cool. At some point I did a solo venture to the far side of the stage. I recognized one of the sound guys as a gent who did sound for my old band Freewheelin' at an outdoor show on Long Beach Island. We were one of five bands on the bill. Nothing big, just Jersey club bands. Skeeter and I kind of hit it off and he asked me if I'd help with a little equipment moving after the show as they were shorthanded. I did and wound up hanging with the crew for the night and helping the next day at another show. That was my only time as a paid "grunt" and I got to wear a cool shirt that said "Crew."

Fast forward some months later to Roosevelt Stadium and there was Skeets running the monitor board for Jerry and the boys. Monitors are the speakers you see on the front of the stage pointing back to the performers. What's coming out of the main speakers should be coming back through the monitors. How bands worked large venues without monitors is beyond me. The Beatles didn't use monitors on their first US tours. Live at the Hollywood Bowl is sans monitors. Ringo would say he'd watched John Lennon's butt going up and down to follow the rhythm.

I got Skeeter's attention and he waved me around to the side and up some stairs to the backstage area. After some pleasantries he gave me a laminated pass and said, "Look like you belong." Like they say to newcomers to the Super Bowl or World Series, "Act like you've been here before." Ok. I can do that. I was sitting on a milk crate staring at the monitor board pretending to look interested. Skeeter was just a grunt for this show but was watching the board for someone who had to disappear for a few minutes. The guy returned, looked at my laminate, gave me the ok sign and I was officially part of the crew. Dang! I could see my buddies out front, but they hadn't noticed me. After about fifteen minutes the Dead took a break and wandered right past me. The backstage area was a little past where I was and the guys were just hanging, having a beer, chatting and other things. I'd get a glance every now and then but after all the antics the Dead had experienced nothing seemed to faze them. Who was I? They didn't know.

But I had a laminate. I must belong. I sat, kept my mouth shut and tried to look like I'd been there before. I ran into Skeeter a few more times before he was killed in a car wreck two years later. He was a good soul and gave me an afternoon I'll never forget. Happy birthday, Jerry. RIP Skeeter.

I was trying to look like I belonged on the egg with Sam and Dave. There was no way to act like I'd been there before. How could I? When I opened my eyes, I was greeted with just one more stunning sight in a litany of stunning sights. The egg was hovering just off the ground on what appeared to be a bog. It was an area not unlike you'd see in the old Sherlock Holmes movies. Kind of murky, wet and misty. I'd been in the Florida Everglades once and this could have been it.

Dave said, "Go explore. Nothing to fear. We'll be back shortly." Oh, that old chestnut, I thought. Well, I was suited up, helmet and all and stepped out of the egg and onto fairly terra firma. Trust, Lyons, trust. They gave a wave and... gone. That was a quick departure.

4

Quiet. Noticeably quiet. The sky was a dark, dark blue and the sun which I could only look at briefly was reddish but surprise, there was another sun. It was smaller but appeared closer somehow and had a reddish tint. I thought for a minute maybe they'd dropped me off back home, but the two suns dispelled that thought. Thin clouds were racing across the sky. I'm not sure what that meant. Rotation speed? Size of the planet?

I started walking. I didn't know if a gizmo had been adjusted on my suit, but the gravity felt like Earth, no.... lighter than earth. I came out of the bog into a lusher savanna type area. There were patches of trees, palm trees. No coconuts that I could see. I was walking through a wide swath of tall, chest high grass. Does that constitute a savanna? I'm not sure. I could see four groups of trees within about a quarter mile. I realized I probably wouldn't be able to hear anything through the helmet. That made me a little nervous. There was a small drop in front of me that led down to a moving river. The water was so clear it looked like running air cascading around black rocks. That must have made a sound, but I couldn't hear it. Everything was similar to Earth, the sky, the river, the trees, yet different, alien. I wanted to take the helmet off to smell the air. They didn't say I couldn't. But I didn't. Following the river for a few hundred yards I took a slight incline back up to the open area. I figured Sam and Dave could find me with the super

GPS and if not, well, I was already instinctively checking for food sources.

I still wasn't sure what the game plan was, what the exit strategy was. Was there an exit strategy? I was committed to the going with the flow thing, but I was getting curious. I've always had a good sense of people, of situations; when to run, when to get ready to run and when to stand my ground. I could tell who to avoid and who'd be a friend for life. Sometimes this would go beyond a sense to a certain knowledge. One particularly strong instance occurred in my sixth-grade classroom.

We were involved in a book sale and had a drawing at the end to see who would win the prize, a stuffed dog. Forty kids put their names in a box. The teacher reached into the box and pulled out a name. I was in the process of shutting the classroom's large, old windows with the classic old-school six-foot window pole. Not an easy task but we all had certain assignments and windows was better than erasers. As Mrs. Burke was pulling out the winning name, I replaced the pole in its hanger and started walking toward her desk. I reached her desk just as she looked up and saw me standing there. Some amused looks. I knew, with a dead-on certainty, that the doggie was coming home with me.

I can't explain it. Four or five other instances have led me to believe that I have somewhat of a gift. But I think we all do, and we just have to recognize it when it presents itself. I also have and have always had a feel for dogs I could approach and those I'd better walk around. I love dogs. And dogs would usually return the sentiment. I can't tell you how many times I'd be in someone's house, in the airport or on the street and made friends with a strange dog. The owner would be surprised 'cause "he doesn't usually like strangers." "I'm no stranger, I'd say, just a friend they hadn't met." I heard that somewhere. I do still have a scar on my hand where I misread a doggie situation when I was about ten. But I came into his space. My bad. Fast forward and I had a good sense of Sam and Dave and this nutty situation. It seemed right. I liked these guys. I trusted these guys. Sense don't fail me now!

The groups of trees seemed strategically placed with seven or eight trees to a group winding in and around each other to a height of twenty or thirty feet. I didn't want to know if there was anything I couldn't see in the grass I was walking through, but it seemed to end about one hundred yards ahead. And end it did. I was standing on the edge of a canyon that would rival our own Grand Canyon. It was magnificent with large striations of blue rock running through it. I could see the river that I'd been following ended as a waterfall flowing over the edge into a raging river below. Raging is the only word that could describe the force of the water I was seeing.

This canyon wasn't nearly as deep as ours, but it felt larger. Like the Grand Canyon, I didn't feel like my eyes could take in the whole thing. And, like the Grand Canyon, the walls and nooks seemed to look a little different every few minutes. Two suns will do that. In most areas the grass went right up to the edge of the great hole but there were a few bare, dirt like places. I pulled up a seat and hung my legs over the side. If I were trying to impress a visitor from beyond Earth, the Grand Canyon wouldn't be a bad place to start. My hosts had picked the perfect spot. I couldn't see the end of the canyon on my left or right but looking across it appeared to continue with grass and patches of trees. I had to remember this. And I was hungry.

I laid down, feet hanging over the edge and stared up at the sky which was now thick with clouds. Man, I wish I could take this helmet off and smell the air. I'll bet there was a wonderful smell of storm and approaching rain in the air. I realized storm, rain and air may not apply here but they were my only frames of reference. The trees and grasses were swaying, the clouds were ripping, and it was time for a daring move. I removed my helmet and took a deep breath of sweet, sweet…. air? I could taste it. That was probably not a smart move, but I was pretty sure I could reset the helmet if I had to. I stood up. I felt a little woozy between the empty stomach and the sweet air which was getting a little sickening. I could hear the river and the wind. I could also hear a rumbling. The "angels were bowling." Thunder. No lightning yet.

There seemed to be a constant in everything I'd seen so far. It was a constant that was hard to put my finger on but the universe, what little I've seen of it, had a theme of sorts. Nothing was completely alien, except for the few Aldairan words I'd heard. There was nothing I'd look at and couldn't relate to or recognize in some way. As of yet the universe was not "queerer than I can suppose." But I'd only seen the "drop in the bucket."

I had to pop the helmet back on. I felt overloaded with oxygen. I heard something; the grass being disturbed by the arrival of the egg. Dave stepped out, took me by the arm and decisively led me back into the egg. He fiddled with my breathing apparatus and I immediately felt normal. I can't say better just normal. He told me that the atmosphere here was too rich and long exposure could get me extremely sick. I wondered why he came out with no helmet and was told that for both of us short periods were ok but not recommended. They liked the smell of fresh air, also. He handed me what resembled an apple. I'd just left the Garden of Eden and I was being handed an apple. How biblical.

"Is there any life here?" I asked. The fruit was soft and delicious. I was hungry.

Dave chimed in," There's bacterial life. And the beginnings of small aquatic life forms. It's a beginning. Life, given a chance, always finds a way." He handed me another apple.

I thought," It's a lot like earth, as was the last place we visited."

"Many are" came the thought back to me.

Dave said," This star system is very healthy. Not all are. This section of our Milky Way (smile) is full of life and potential life." Wow, were we all brothers and sisters after all? Again, I got that, "you're starting to get it," look. I slipped into my seat which conveniently appeared every time I was ready to sit down. There was a tremendous flash of lightening as we shot straight up and into blackness. Watching the storm from above was just cool. "Can we stay here for a second?" I asked. Again, that grin and we slowed to a stop.

"Let us know." I heard. Talk, thoughts, it was all becoming very understandable and normal. I was getting the hang of this.

5

I was told that what I saw as a second sun was really a large moon reflecting the sunlight of this star, our neighbor, Alpha Centauri. Alpha Centauri had three stars, or two, depending on to whom you spoke, similar to the Pluto/planet discussion. The moon was close enough to be seen during the day. I couldn't help thinking that any member of Earth's scientific community would have obviously been a better fit for this experience. They'd know what questions to ask. Those meetings would come, I supposed. Ok boys, let's ride. (too familiar?)

I thought Alpha Centauri had, as far as we knew, one planet. So far, I've seen two inhabited planets. I was told this system is much larger than we thought and has five planets and a number of moons. The number of planets by our standards has become a very fluid proposition. We were headed to the farthest out planet. About fifteen minutes later at cruising speed the gray ball came into view. The first thing I noticed was three moons. My amateur take away was that the planet was smaller than Earth and mesmerizing in a dead kind of way. We zipped to and hovered by one of the moons. On a close up, maybe fifty miles, a huge chasm seemed to divide the moon in half. We circled and indeed, it did go all the way around the moon. It was as if two halves smashed into each other and stuck. A galactic wall. Up and away.

We headed toward the planet and kept descending stopping over an ice cap. A small river was running down one side. The liquid was a bluish, cold looking color. It felt like there was a thin atmosphere with stars visible even though I was sure it was daytime. All very confusing. I was beginning to rely on impressions rather than facts. We started to pull away just as I spotted a small lizard like creature slip into the river. I looked at Sam and Dave. Life always finds a way.

We continued at a moderate speed about one hundred feet off the ground. Every now and then there'd be a patch of brown or green otherwise the surface was barren. I wondered how the lizard creature survived. The first visitors to Earth would have wondered the same thing if they landed in Death Valley and saw a slithering snake or a Gila monster. How can anything survive on this barren planet, they'd think. If they took the time to continue, they'd come across the lush, vibrant Amazon rain forest, or the vastness of the oceans.

I remembered the parable of the six blind men and the elephant. Each grabbed a different part of the elephant, ear, tusk, knee, tail, trunk, torso and tail. And each came away with a different idea of what an elephant was. They were all right and they were all wrong.

We banked right and headed down to the edge of a large lake. Steam or something was rising from it. We stopped and I followed Sam out to the surface. It was not a lake but a large hole, maybe three or five miles across. I don't know what created the steam or where it was coming from. Sam pulled out a small flat board type apparatus, stood on it and disappeared into the steam. That looked like fun. I looked back into the egg and Dave was busy on the iPad. I was poking around at the chunky, dark ground at the edge of the "lake" and was surprised by a flock of...birds? Tiny black birds, hundreds of them, flew by, over and around me. For about thirty seconds I was frozen in the middle of this moving black mass. Help? The cloud of birds rapidly thinned out and also disappeared into the steam. I hoped Sam would be ok. He came out a minute or two later. He asked if I'd "seen the flight." Thought impressions. I said I'd seen the flight. He was standing on the board that was very much like the hoverboard in "Back to The Future."

I was still waiting to see something really alien. So far everything I'd witnessed, as cool and stunning and wow factorish as they were, could still be recognized as having a basis in my earthly reality. It was beginning to look like everything took the same developmental trajectory. I realized that, like the blind men, I was making a supposition on an extremely limited experience. Hey, I'm only human. The "hoverboard" was collapsed and Sam put it in a pocket on his suit. The collapsible board, like the shrinking iPad, was interesting but not outside the realm of possibility.

I think if the idea of an automobile were laid out to the actual Benjamin Franklin, he could probably get the concept. Small explosions turn shafts connected to wheels and you're on your way. But could he understand the ones and zeros and bits and bytes of our modern computers? That would take a leap of faith. The internet, movies and the world of germs would probably be "queerer than he could suppose." And we were off again. Sleep.

I wondered what my hosts ultimate job was. Were they preparing me to pave the way for first contact or just blowing the mind of a typical Earth guy whom they divined had an interest in what or who was out there? I really hoped this was the beginning of a beautiful friendship.

6

Sam, Dave and I had our spots in the egg. We were in overdrive judging by the stars dripping by. After I came to Sam and Dave began peppering me with questions. They were mainly interested in the "nature of man," our obsession with love, war, and the seeming lack of interest in the welfare of our earthly brothers and sisters. It wasn't judgmental or condemning in any way, just a curiosity. That was tough to explain. But I tried. Emotions, which they lacked, were at the root of all of it. Love and hate. Yin and yang. Comedy and tragedy. They were also interested in our love of the arts; music, reading for enjoyment, sculpture, plays, movies etc. Also, our interest in sports, recreational and professional. I was telling them these are all things that make us feel. Smacking a line drive feels good. Hearing "Walk Away Renee" makes me think of a high school girlfriend who broke my heart. Sad. Watching "Psycho" makes you feel scared. Seeing Michelangelo's "Pieta" at the New York World's Fair made me feel humbled, serene. Listening to Martin Luther King's "I have a dream" speech makes me feel hopeful and proud. Dancing to Motown makes me feel happy. Human emotions. The Aldairan emotions were returning, slowly. They put their return to the emotional maelstrom at twenty five percent.

"Just enough to get into trouble," I said. They didn't get it. I told them of my conversation with Dr Franklin regarding procreation within our own race and why it wouldn't work. I thought we'd eventually have to go through what they did. They understood. They both looked at me and said, clearly," Don't you see? We. You. Us. We're all related."

"Stardust." I said. That provoked an actual smile. An emotion. Things were falling into place.

There's any number of movies, books or stories told around the campfire that probe the possibility of a universal connection. There's the Twilight Zone in which, I think it's Charles Bronson, is an astronaut stranded on a distant planet. He meets a frightened Elizabeth Montgomery who is apparently the sole survivor of global catastrophe. After some false starts they decide to move through life as a team. He's trying to get her to understand his name, Adam. Her name, of course is Eve. "What should we call this place? "Bronson wants to know. Eve grabs a handful of dirt and grunts something almost intelligible. Bronson nods, "Earth it is." BAM!

Then there's the one where the two families who work for the space agency decide to hightail it out of town before the inevitable nuclear holocaust. They manage to fight their way past the guards, get into the saucer and vacate the premises. On the way one of the kids inquires where they're headed. Dad points to a star and says," The third planet to the left. It's called.... Earth. BAM again! And in the classic final scene of Planet of the Apes, Charlton Heston, who's been through the mill at this point, spots a broken Statue of Liberty on the beach and finally realizes that he's been on Earth the whole time. "Damn you all to hell!" We want to know. We're curious.

The theories that we are ancestors of a long-gone Martian race or that a meteor, comet or some outside source collided with Earth and started the life cycle are a couple of popular ones.

We want to belong to something. We need each other, someone. It's a human condition. I like solitude. I need solitude. I'm fine being alone. As I said earlier, give me a ball, a glove and a wall or steps and I could amuse myself for hours. A cross country trip, solo vacations, an afternoon with a book, guitar or movie and I'm good. But sooner or later I, we, need companionship. Sooner or later we'll want to share that gorgeous sunset with someone. Or share an appetizer. Or hold hands during a movie. Or slow dance with someone you love.

Then there is the simple and most widely accepted ideas. Big Bang. Something triggered the granddaddy of all explosions, matter congealed and over billions of years, galaxies, stars, planets and eventually life came into being. Or the one that the nuns in St Mary's drilled into me that God created the heavens and the earth in seven days, seven days being a relative term. Adam soon appeared in the Garden of Eden followed by Eve. They ate the forbidden fruit, got thrown out of the Garden and so humanity began. I never had a problem mixing God with the Big Bang. God clapped his hands (Big Bang) sat back and watched. I believe in God or some sort of spiritual caretaker that watches over us. I've also thought he/she is more of a hands-off kind of parent. That would explain a lot. I pray anyway. The life after life experiences are always an interesting read. One similar takeaway is that time over there is more fluid than here. Eternity, everything, is now. Don't stress it. It's just that ten, fifty, two hundred million years may be two weeks to God. Just a thought. And who really knows? I'd get a closer look at that later.

7

The life I'd observed already, in this tiny part of our Milky Way, just a galactic heartbeat away, was surprising and, at the same time, not. I always felt the universe was bristling with life. Given its immensity, number of stars, galaxies and planets it shouldn't be surprising but seeing it close up, it is. How much more is out there. And how many civilizations are the Aldairans, even in their limited travels, aware of?

Dave handed me something that resembled a piece of beef jerky. It tasted like cake. Weird, I know. It's kind of unsettling biting into jerky and tasting cake. But it had a pleasant taste. I asked for another and Dave passed me one. I felt like I'd been asleep. Again. Sam confirmed that I'd been asleep for five hours. I'm not a great sleeper and it dawned on me that I was regularly passing out in the egg. How was that happening? I thought.

"We're helping you," Dave said. He pointed to the gizmo on my chest. Sneaky.

"It's not sleep," Sam said. "More of a stasis or coma." "Suspended animation?" I asked, using my best Saturday afternoon science fiction reference. Two head shakes were the answer.

We slowed, then stopped. We were again in the cosmic void between stars. As empty as the space between planets can feel, the star/sun supplies a warmth, if not physically, emotionally. You're close to something. Out here we're free of any pull or fields of a star. We're on our own. Focusing on that can tend to freak you out. Freak me out. I didn't focus on it and again invoked my mantra of trust. Sam and Dave were both eating. Good to know. What about sleep, I wondered?

"We sleep," came the reply. Also, good to know. They asked if I was ready to see their home and that we were only a few hours away. I HAD to get one of these eggs. Yes, I was ready to see their home.

I was standing against the wall of the egg. Once again, I was amazed at the proximity of us to that. The lights dimmed and the feeling of standing in space was vertigo inspiring. Once I realized I might be taking another spacewalk, it was on. Sam handed me a helmet which I was rather good at popping on by now. They were going to power down and rest. You would think that telepathic communication would be a mixed jumble of noise. It wasn't. It worked perfectly. I don't know how it worked but just what was supposed to be conveyed was conveyed. It was beautiful. I hoped I could hang on to some of that. The chairs relaxed into a soft incline and the guys stretched out.

"If you need us, reach out," Sam said. I wasn't sure what to do. Sam touched something on the iPad and motioned me to step out. A deep breath and step out I did!

8

With an authority that came from I don't know where I had really stepped out. I was moving away from the egg at a pretty good clip. The only way I had any sense of movement was watching the shrinking of the egg. Once again, I was admiring, even as I was disappearing into the cosmos, the beautiful simplicity of the Aldairan craft. I wondered if this was the first vehicle the kids on Aldair received from their parents, like the 1967 VW convertible I got from my cousin when I was seventeen. It was free. All I had to do was tow it home to Piscataway from Newark, sink thirty-seven dollars in it to get it running and I was off, most of the time. Occasionally the troops had to line up in the Piscataway Township High School parking lot to give me a push but then.... I was off. The Aldairan kids would really be off. (Now no visiting other galaxies. We want you staying within our own solar system or you'll be in big trouble!)

I did a quick check of my suit, and I'll say it again, I gotta get one of these, and all seemed cool. When I looked up the egg was gone. Or, I guess the egg was right where I left it and I was gone. With no frame of reference, I had absolutely no sense of movement, again. I could see stars but rather than feeling I was within them, I felt like an outsider looking in. The space we were covering in the time we were covering it was mind boggling. I was getting spoiled. "A few hours to your planet?! But it's only in the next star system! Are we there yet?" And we are adaptable creatures.

On the one hand, it's, not depressing, but a realization, that in twenty, fifty, eighty years we may have the technology to send a craft out that will be able to catch up with Voyager, complete its mission and pick it up on the way back to Earth, particularly if we can elicit a shortcut or two from the Aldairans. Does this mean we should stop NASA from inventing, creating, dreaming and doing? No. As humans we simply can't. Recording digitally sure beats four track tape but if I didn't learn the lessons on tape, I would have been behind the eight ball when digital rolled around. Should you wait to get the next incarnation of the iPhone or laptop? I guess you can but at some point, you must jump in. Its' a long-connected road from the massive computers that took up entire rooms to the iPad. Learning each step along the way just makes sense. It's a learning curve we've all had to endure. Just when I think I'm out it pulls me back in!

Again I must reference the great Rod Serling. An astronaut was to embark on a mission that would take him out to deep space. He'd be put into a state of suspended animation, wakened to complete his mission, be put back into suspended animation and return to Earth thirty years from when he left. He wouldn't have aged except for the short time it took him to do what he had to do before he returned to sleep. Unfortunately, as he was preparing to leave, he met a woman and fell in love. It was not to be as he'd return thirty years her junior. What to do? Fast forward thirty years. Our man lands and as he's exiting his ship, we see his girlfriend running up. She hasn't changed! The suspended animation technology had been perfected and was available to the public. She opted in. As she looks up to the door of the craft her face tells it all. Our intrepid traveler exits thirty years older. He'd not gone the suspended animation route but endured the thirty-year mission awake and looking forward to seeing his love. They were both heartbroken but there you have it. A short commiseration and they go their separate ways. To add insult to injury the technology needed to do his mission was advanced a few years after he left so there was no need for him to even be out there. Why they didn't just tell him to turn around is anybody's guess. It wouldn't have made much of a story is the easy answer. Mr. Serling always wanted to leave us with something to think about.

The feeling of serenity and all's well was like nothing I'd felt before or since. I wondered if Sam and Dave were doctoring my oxygen a smidge to keep me on this calm path. Laid back is a phrase that's always been associated with me, but this was a little mystifying. I completely turned myself over to everything and anything these guys wanted to do. Even before my first step from my back lawn into the egg I got how special this was, that even if I couldn't return or met my maker in the process it would be worth it. And hopefully somehow, someway friends and family would be aware of it. I didn't want to become one of the Bermuda Triangle entries. Whatever happened to......? That's sad for everyone. Closure, as painful as it can be, is necessary.

That got me thinking about Linda again. If I could get a message to her, I'd feel a whole lot better. And I'll bet she would, too. This wasn't like staying out with the boys and forgetting to call. She tended to worry and this situation certainly gave her reason to. She had a lot on her plate. She had to explain my disappearance for a few days. Or she could do nothing and just wait. I wasn't sure at this point how long I'd been gone. When I returned would everyone I know, and love be thirty years older? Would I return? I still didn't really know exactly what this was all about. Dr. Ben dispensed the "Love your neighbor, we are all one" philosophy. That was good. I'm glad to deliver that message. But was there more, something else? Maybe I didn't want to know. I'd find out about contacting Earth.

9

Time was an unknown quantity. My internal clock had quit working. When things were popping, I was super alert. On down time I felt like I could drop off in a snap. I was floating during down time between stars. I fell asleep. I had a sensation of soft rolling like on a child's roller coaster at a county carnival. I snapped awake and I was gently moving up and down, as was the space around me. Space was rippling. What was happening? I was too mesmerized to be afraid, I guess. How can I describe what materialized in front of me? It was a giant cartoonish head, as if someone had drawn the outline of a five- or six-foot head complete with eyes, nose and mouth. Space and stars were visible through the apparition. It was smiling, blinking and staring at me intently. It was a more human looking Porky Pig, a pen and ink caricature of what a human would look like with swinish qualities. It felt childlike and non-threatening. I followed its gaze to my right and here came the egg, but it was a different, larger egg. Pig man was laughing. He seemed to be enjoying himself. The gentle ripple came back into our space and it vanished.

Had I been dreaming? I looked over and Sam was floating toward me. I could see inside the larger egg and recognized Gidget. There were six or seven other folks. People? ETs? What do I call them at this point?

Sam grabbed me by both arms and looked directly into my eyes. "Did you see that?" I said, a little too loud. Sam looked over at the last of the disappearing ripple and guided me back and into the super egg. It was about three times the size of our craft and had a few more amenities. Sam checked my chest doohickey and I removed my helmet. I said hello to Gidget and was once again the center of attention among the other Aldairans. They all seemed excited, more than just to see me.

Sam was still looking at me like a concerned friend or brother. "I'm ok," I said. "But what the hell was that?" A large chatter erupted. One of the Aldairans I recognized from the Mother Ship walked over to me and said, almost giddily," We don't know. They pop up one or two at a time every now and then. They seem interested and curious but non-threatening. We think they're from either a different time or possibly another dimension given the way space is disrupted on their arrival and departure. They don't seem to have any interest in communicating. The truth is, we just don't know."

That was all communicated telepathically with the requisite British accent, eyes blinking uncontrollably out of sync. That still seemed strange. Not quite as strange as the time/dimension traveling pig man cartoon face, but still, a little weird. This guy had a familiarity to him. He looked like Ringo! His nose had a fullness to it that the others lacked. I wonder if he heard "Hey, quit breathin' up all the air," a lot? I don't know if it's just me but again, to me, everyone looks like someone else. Many times, I've said to people, "Anyone ever tell you that you look like.....?" My personal bad. So, we had Gidget and Ringo and Sam and Dave just for convenience. Ringo's nose wasn't bulbous, just larger than I was seeing on the Aldairans. Still small by human standards. I thought I heard them recognizing each other by name but I just couldn't grab it. I asked if they could travel to other dimensions or other times and they said dimensionally, no, but regarding time travel, they don't travel in time but time travels to them. I'm not sure who said that or maybe it was a group thought.

"We'll show you more about that when we get home," Sam said loudly and clearly. What did that mean? Time travel? I also had to find out about this dimension thing. Other universes? The stuff comic books are made of. The subject was never revisited. Again, I assumed once we and they sat down and hashed it all out all these questions that I forgot to follow up on would be thoroughly answered. That's what I thought.

It seemed that this crew was heading to Aldair but Sam and I would be heading back to egg junior to continue the trip with Dave. I kinda liked this slick ride. But ya gotta dance with who brung ya. Dave cruised into view and the two eggs seemed to mesh into each other. I gave a goodbye wave to Gidget and the crew as Sam and I walked into our egg. Everything was becoming so normal. I took a seat. Dave gave me my iPad. I expanded it and got to work. Sam and Dave were standing and intently chatting. They were really vamping in that cool sounding Aldairan language. Dave looked over at me.

"I hope you're not talking about me," I said.

Sam said, "We're talking about all of us." Sam walked into the mother egg. He came back in a few minutes and said we'd be riding to Aldair together. About one third of our egg was inside Gadget's, kind of melted together. We could walk from one to the other. Very symbiotic, like a small mother/daughter home. When will the coolness end?

Everyone had a job to do. I had to catch up on my note taking. Gidget brought me something that resembled a hamburger. She asked, "Is this close?"

I said, "Close enough, I'm sure. Thank you." I took a bite of a Chocolatey/potatoey and very salty hamburger. I ate it and drank the container of water she left with it. It was water. Everyone was noshing on something. I saw a comfortable looking seat in the larger egg and asked Dave if I could wander over there. He gave me a wave and I settled into a recliner that basically wrapped itself around me as a small table came up from my feet and stopped at my lap in a perfect incline. A dark beige shade rose behind where I was and covered the back half of mother egg and half of the front. Just a large front windshield remained. (Flaps down. Seats in the upright position.) My seat reminded me of one of those sixties' chairs, usually white, that looked like a half egg on a stand. You could spin while listening to music on interior speakers. Unlike my star chair they weren't very comfortable, but the coolness factor made up for it. Lava lamp not included. I figured the trip may take a while and I had a lot of catching up to do.

We were now farther out than Voyager. At last look Voyager was preparing to leave our solar system and enter interstellar space. And still working! Kudos to the amazing minds that put those things together. All the gadgets work as long and well as they were designed to and then keep on ticking. And here I am, a shlub who had to take a school year and summer school, then with extra help finally got the concept of geometry, hanging out noodling on an extraterrestrial iPad a star system and a half farther out than Voyager. Albert Einstein, Stephen Hawking, Carl Sagan or any number of scientific luminaries should be sitting in this seat trying to digest a chocolate salt burger. But it was me. Where's the justice? I felt a soft push, looked out the front windshield and the stars were once again like raindrops on a windshield. Overdrive.

10

This was fun. It was interesting, frightening, enlightening and mystifying but overall, it was fun! As an adult when do we really have fun? I mean that sledding down a hill, first drop on the roller coaster, body surfing the perfect wave, whoopee kind of fun. Probably not often. Rolling out of an airplane at ten thousand feet attached to a guy whose last words on exiting were, "We're probably not gonna die," was fun. I try to enjoy little things. I try to stop at batting cages or driving ranges when I come across them. If I see a cool trail leading into the woods and have time I'll investigate. Learning and putting songs together and playing my guitar, especially in a crowded bar is fun. But this? This was fun.

Sometimes we try to force fun. New Year's Eve is famous for that. I remember one New Year's with three or four of my Piscataway pals. We covered a slew of parties trying to have fun. It wasn't happening. Around ten o' clock someone suggested going to NYC. We hopped on a train and made it to Times Square around 11:45. It was 1969 -70. You could do that then.

We hung out for a while, caught a bus back to New Brunswick, had a great time on the bus with a bunch of new friends and said good night. That was entertaining. In 1976 my old band Freewheelin' opened up for "Kinderhook Creek" at Somerset County College. Later that year we opened up for "Sauce" at the Strand Theater in Plainfield. Looking out at that balcony brought back memories. That whole year was fun.

One Saturday night in 1970 when I was a freshman at the University of Texas at El Paso, I learned a valuable lesson in the art of having fun. I rolled back into my dorm around eleven o' clock. We had several Asian students on my floor and I was friendly with most of them, even though they were always wrecking the academic curve. I was walking by a room, saw the door open and stuck my head in. I don't remember the gent's name, but he was, relatively speaking, an older guy, maybe early twenties. His English was shaky, but we could communicate. My buddy Kelly, another Jersey boy, and I had been out "hitching for chicks." That was something we'd come up with out of boredom. We would walk up to the main drag, stick our thumbs out and would only get in the car with women, hopefully two or more. Once we made our intentions known they'd either throw us out and take off in a huff or show the two rubes from NJ some of the sights of El Paso. Maybe we'd come home with a phone number or two. Man, that sounds chauvinistic, shallow and immature. But I guess I was chauvinistic, shallow and immature and refuse to apologize for anything I did before the age of twenty-five.

My Asian friend invited me in. We exchanged pleasantries and he chuckled at my Saturday night antics. I asked him if he'd had a nice night. He said, and I've never forgotten this, "Oh yes. I have wonderful time. I write a letter to my girlfriend." He looked so happy. And I felt kind of small. Fun. An important life lesson I've never forgotten.

I woke up with the iPad on the table in front of me and a full bladder. Real sleep or induced sleep I don't know. The sides of the egg had been pulled back to wherever they get pulled back to and we were surrounded by stars, the black of space and, mama loosha, a beautiful blue sphere that could be a twin to earth. Aldair was slowly coming into view. I got up and walked into the smaller egg. I asked Dave if there was a bathroom on board and he said, "Just go." Sam smiled that smile that said either "that's cute" or "what an idiot." I really couldn't tell which. I gotta get one of these suits. I was up against the window taking in the sight of the blue marble when I heard, in unison, "Welcome to Aldair."

[Intermission]

**

This is a blog entry of mine from a few years back. It popped up at an interesting time. Or maybe.... just the right time.

I'm gettin' itchy to meet a galactic neighbor. The time feels right. Don't ask me why. The question of extraterrestrial life comes up fairly regularly in my conversations. I guess because I probably instigate it. The last two or three times it's come up I was met with the response, "I don't think there's anyone out there." That's amazing to me...because I'm so convinced they ARE out there. Maybe it's all those Saturday afternoons watching pods turn into people or trips to a Forbidden Planet or even laughing at Plan 9 From Outer Space. Hey, even an eight-year-old kid can see they changed Bela Lugosi's mid flick. And now it's day.... whoops.... now it's night, uh oh.... day again. Or maybe it's the late-night radio shows I've been running into. Ninety percent of that conversation I don't buy into. I can't say they're wrong. I always say, and will continue to say, ANYTHING'S possible. I just.... don't buy into most of it. I'm not even sure we've ever been observed or visited. I'm just sure they're out there. All those great sci fi movies, as cool as they were, always left me a little cold. I mean, I wanted them to land in my back yard.

Then the question comes up, "Well, why haven't they visited us?" The simple answer is I don't know. No one does. But I have a couple of theories. One is distance. Earth like planets have been discovered a few stars away from us. Ten....fifteen years ago the big question was, "Are there any other planets out there?" Now we know there are. Many. That doesn't mean there's any kind of life out there.... but it doesn't mean there isn't, either. But to get to the closest one, traveling at or near the speed of light, is a generational trip. And that's just tooling around in our own cosmic neighborhood. And the ability to reach anything close to the speed of light is a long way off. Talk to Einstein. So, barring the invention of warp drives or wormhole shortcuts or inter dimensional pathways, it may simply be a matter of leapfrogging our way across the galaxy; a colony here, move on, a colony there, move on, etc. And once we get done with the two hundred billion stars in our galaxy, we can move on to the two hundred billion stars in each of the two hundred billion other galaxies. That' a lot of planets, man. And take these numbers with a grain of salt. Give or take a few billion either way.

My other theory is maybe they've been watching and observing for a long time but have no desire to interact. Could it be we're.... boring? Maybe it's that Star Trek prime directive thing where they can't interfere with a species' natural evolution. Or they're just sizing us up, sittin' back and watching.... seeing if we're gonna make the cut. Maybe whoever's in charge of this whole eternal *universe thing set it up so we CAN'T reach each other. He's given us the tools to cruise around our own cosmic block but no further, as if to say, "Look around, have fun, but tend to your own garden." You can almost see the girl's camp across the lake...but not quite. Curiosity, the latest Mars rover, took off this morning. It's exciting stuff. But TOO SLOW!!! Can someone please invent impulse power NOW?!*

I love watching Nova or tales about the evolution of the universe on the History Channel but the frustrating thing is it always turns out the same. Maybe they're there. Maybe they're not. It's like watching the guys chasing the ghosts. Just show me video of a ghost standing there, wouldja. Not something in the dark at the end of the room for a second and a half that's probably a reflection or a shadow. I guess they can hear it saying "Get Out," but all I hear is static. And I've got a wild imagination. I know I heard John say, "I buried Paul" at the end of Strawberry Fields. When I was fifteen that was a head turner, till I found out he meant Paul was buried in the mix of the album. Dang, skunked again. So, we seem to think they're out there.... but....... the old back and forth.

That doesn't stop me from going out at night and throwing out an open invitation to the universe. So far, no response. I don't think anything landed in Roswell, I don't think there's been any alien abductions...or autopsies. I don't think the government knows any more than anyone else. And if they do.... quit worrying about the panic in the street's scenario. We can handle it. I think.

This quote has been attributed to a few different folks, Isaac Asimov among them. I like it. "The universe is not only stranger than we can imagine, it's stranger than we can imagine." Put that in your phaser and fire it.   Peace

Part 5

**

1

So, if I remembered correctly, we were at the third star out from our sun. You know that feeling when you're on vacation, or on a business trip and you're far, far away from home? That distance between familiarity and here, wherever that may be, seems massive. You picture family and friends doing what they do and a touch of homesickness creeps in. I had that feeling now. Squared. I also needed a bathroom. My suit wasn't ready for what was coming. Dave directed me to a small bathroom on mother egg even though he said that was not necessary. Their system absorbs all solid food with no waste and mine should too. We'll see. It was like the bathroom on the Mother Ship, which I guess is universal and all was well.

The bathroom had a window that looked out into space. Aldair was filling up the view. I touched the window and it turned into a mirror. I thought back to the Three Stooges. They were in a heck of a fix. Curly says, "I'm too young to die. I'm too young. I'm too handsome. (looks in the mirror) Yikes! Well, I'm too young." My reflection looked foreign, a little off. I'm not a great looking guy anyway but I looked.... alien. We resembled the Aldairans enough, but a second glance would be warranted if you saw one behind you in the checkout line. Maybe you wouldn't think alien. Maybe you'd think visitor from a foreign land. Looking into the mirror, which I never enjoy even on my best day, I saw that I was the alien. I touched the mirror again and the void popped back up.

I came back out and the eggs was 'a buzzin'. Gidget and Ringo were speaking to someone on a large screen TV. I walked over and the guy on the screen did a double take. He looked like Charlie Watts, drummer for the Stones. A pastier Charlie, and Charlie's pretty pasty. The Aldairans all had the same light, almost transparent skin tone, some a shade darker than others. I waved. Gidget turned, put her arm in my arm and did an introductory "Ta Daaa" gesture. Her arm felt like a long twig. Mine felt short and stumpy. I don't know why nature elongated their limbs, but it did. That would earn a second look in the checkout line. Maybe. Charlie waved back. No smile. That was the first uncomfortable vibe I'd felt to date. I backed off and crossed over to egg junior. Sam and Dave were also watching a screen. It was an

Aldairan conference call with Charlie, Sam and Dave and Gidget and Ringo. I pulled up a chair and got back to iPaddin' till the next call to action.

2

I was taking notes and enjoying the view. We seemed to be circling Aldair or maybe it was quickly rotating below us. I never quite understood how that worked, the space station, orbit thing. Those were the kind of questions you had to ask when you were a kid. The "Why is the sky blue?" kind of questions. I think I could fake my way through a why is the sky blue; sunlight hitting the atmosphere, breaking into spectrum colors with blue being the most dominant. That's my shot. But I was always fascinated at how things work in space, like sound, weightlessness, how things would enter or leave the earth, what would happen if this or that occurred, how and where an orbit would begin, what does the sun look like from space etc. I was getting the answers to some of these questions firsthand.

Occasionally I would drive a guy who worked at a local observatory. We'd have some great conversations, at least from my perspective. I'd usually start out with, "I should really know this by now but...." He was very patient and would then pepper me with music questions. Questions he should have the answers to by now. We'd always come back to "are they out there (we both assumed they were) and when will we meet them." I got some answers for ya!

I'd been ignoring my note taking and staring down at Aldair. We'd circled (orbited?) it once or twice and it was becoming familiar. There were two large land masses, a smaller land mass and maybe a dozen islands of different sizes. Aldair looked to have about a fifty-fifty water to land ratio. I just noticed we were going over the poles instead of around what would be the equator. Why? I don't know. The axis seemed more severe that Earth's and I spotted a small land mass on the southern pole. We really needed a scientist here. I was just wingin' it.

We were getting closer on every go around and now the Mother Ship had joined us. It appeared to be the one we'd been on earlier but who knew? Sam joined me. He asked if I'd be willing to stay aboard mother and come down to Aldair tomorrow, whatever tomorrow was. He said I could stay at his home or at a "visitors' station." A Twilight Zone thought crossed my mind. I really hoped the visitor's station wasn't an interstellar zoo. Again, these came through as impressions that I understood and not complete sentences. I got the drift.

"How long have we been gone?" I asked.

He said," Two Earth days" It seemed like a month. I asked if we'd be heading back anytime soon and he said whenever I wanted. I wanted to know if he or anyone would be coming down to Earth with me for a "Take me to your leader moment." He told me they were discussing it but maybe not at this time.

"You tell them," He said in perfect British accented English. He sensed my disappointment; said he'd see me below and left. Small egg detached from mother egg and we headed to the Mother Ship on the next go round. It was Dave and me pulling into Mother.

3

This was not the same Mother Ship we'd met up with earlier. On closer inspection it was much smaller, about half the size of the earlier craft. This vessel would have seemed huge had I not experienced the other one first. We entered from below and came up into a receiving or docking area. There were just two levels of ports and all, but two ports were taken. We docked. It looked like every port had an exit directly in front of it, like spokes on a wheel. We exited and started walking straight ahead down a hallway. About fifty feet down we stopped. A door whooshed open on my left, we walked in and I was home for the night. Dave walked to a closet type area and pointed to a number of suits, then walked me to the bathroom area, waved his hand in front of a patch on the wall and a steamy, vaporous substance erupted.

"Shower?" I inquired.

"Shower," came the reply. Hmmm, three days, I thought. Is he trying to tell me something? Was I emitting an aroma? Back in the main area he pointed to the white button and "plate" on the desk, which I recognized as the magic food machine, a shelf with chilled water bottles and basically we were in a room that was a clone of my earlier room. Dave made the ok, see ya later sign and I said, "Thanks." A wry smile and he departed. Again, I had that feeling that there was a joke I wasn't in on. Trust.

I stripped off the suit and went into the bathroom. I punched the patch on the wall and the eruption began. I stuck my hand in. No real sensation besides a light pressure. I stepped in. There were no soaps, shampoos, washcloths or any of the amenities one would expect from a first-class hotel. I will be speaking to the concierge. I laughed out loud, and the echo took me by surprise. Bathroom reverb is universal. "In the still.... of the ni – ite." Cool. This felt good. Energizing. I stood in the mist for a while slowly turning and wiping. I hit the patch again and the steam stopped. This was not a bathtub/shower area, just a space on an area of blank wall where steam like vapor shot out at a perfect angle, as if it's target could be recognized. I looked around for a towel and realized I didn't need one. I was dry and never felt so clean. Even my hair was dry.

The futuristic toilet and sink were there, and I spotted a small depression above and to the right of the sink. I hadn't noticed that in the other bathroom. And why a toilet? For the old school folks? I touched the depression on the wall and the space didn't open as much as fade to a three by three area full of stuff. Most I didn't recognize; some were slightly familiar, and the brush could have come out of any Walgreens. I grabbed and brushed and like everything else there was a little something extra, a simultaneous brush and massage. The mirror, like Earth mirrors, did nothing to flatter me so I went to the closet, grabbed a galactic robe instead of the wet suit and I was set.

I walked over to the food thingy, the white button next to the plant, and touched it. A menu came up in the air right in front of me. It had to have been custom made for me, and Dr Franklin. I pushed chicken salad sandwich and a slight vibration later in the receiving space appeared a tuna fish sandwich! So, they weren't perfect. And that was a good tuna fish sandwich. I washed it down with some bottled water off a shelf that kept it at a perfect chill and sat down to continue my diary. I leaned back and the chair conformed perfectly. I was clean, fed and comfortable.

When I was a kid and if we'd be, for instance, on the beach at the Jersey shore drying off from a dip and enjoying one of Mom's baloney sandwiches, extra sand of course, at some point my father would say, "I wonder what the poor people are doing today." We were solidly just a middle-class family, but we could be fooled into thinking otherwise. It's amazing what a full belly, a warm summer sun and the Four Seasons blaring out of a transistor radio can do to your reality. I had to laugh. I wondered, just like dad, what were the poor people doing today. I sat at the desk, touched and expanded the port hole and for the next hour or so jotted down thoughts and impressions and watched Aldair slowly turn below me. Tomorrow. You're only a day away.

4

I don't think I remembered moving to the bed but as a soft chime brought me around that's where I was. I got up, went to the door and waved my hands up and down and around to no avail. I said, "Come in" and the door swung wide. There stood Dave and something else. We were NOT in Kansas anymore. Remember that thing I said before about not seeing anything really alien, that I had a frame of reference for everything I'd seen? Well, shut my mouth. I made a weird sound, tripped backwards over my feet and wound up on my butt staring up at E freakin' T! Dave stepped in and looked concerned. I waved him off, got up and said something like "Homina homina." ET stepped in behind him. "Don't be alarmed. She's not here." Dave said. "She's three decks up. This is what you might call a hologram but not exactly. She wanted to meet you." A hologram video phone call, I thought.

"Yes! Yes!" I heard.

She was...um.... tall, over six feet with large, mesmerizing almond shaped eyes. Oh yeah, and she looked like an ant, an ant with the large ET head we've seen in the movies. She, it, appeared curious, staring at me in a childlike, very curious way. She was smiling. I think. Her eyes worked independently and were moving around in an odd manner. She had skinny arms and legs, a small thin torso and a large butt type area, like a bee's stinger or that thing an ant has. Or maybe it was just a fanny pack. I don't know. She looked like the result of a mating between the cool alien at the end of *Close Encounters of the Third Kind* and an ant, leaning more towards the ET. Where's an etymologist when you need one?!

Dave told me this was a female. She was from a civilization that came from a flourishing moon in the Aldairan star system and somewhere beyond before that. Technologically they were more advanced than us and had been interacting with the Aldairans for about seventy-five years. Their "enlightenment" was in full swing and progressing rapidly. The video hologram was for mine and "her" safety. No one was sure about contagions and why take a chance. I was about to say something to ant lady when Dave said I was at a slight disadvantage as she'd seen humans, in person or otherwise but this was my first glimpse at a truly alien figure. She looked at Dave and at an unspoken cue faded out. Dave said this would be another piece of information I could bring back. I said I thought I'd heard that the Aldairans were the only life in this system. Dave said Aldair was the only planet with life. These creatures were from a planet's moon. He said a few of the moon's in our system will eventually surprise us. Once I got used to the ant lady's surprising visual aspect, I thought she was quite stunning, in an alien kind of way. I hoped my how do you do from the prone position wasn't offensive.

He'd used the word creature. What was the context there, I wondered? Moon, planets, giant ants, hologram video calls. My head hurt. Dave said relax, have some food and he'd be back a little later to go down to Aldair. He started to walk out, turned around and said, "Are you alright?" I think he said healthy, but I heard a feeling of compassionate concern.

I said, "All things considered, I'm fine. I'm looking forward to seeing your home." He left. I still had the bathrobe on. I went for a new wetsuit feeling pretty much the buffoon.

5

I was at an absolute loss for passage of time. I guess I had grabbed a short nap till Dave and ant lady dropped by. I never slept like this. I slept, but fifteen- or twenty-minutes winding down time was the norm. Here I was dropping off every time I sat or lay down. Maybe it was the air. I'd never thought about the air regulator gizmo. It was still on my suit. I guess the air in my room was managed for me. Or did things just automatically happen, a computerized guardian angel? I was all in and hoped, trusted, for the best.

I've always been good at sizing up situations, that sixth sense thing I mentioned earlier. In 1970 during Easter break my pal Butch and I decided to hitch hike to Hollywood, Butch to see a girl, and me to have an adventure and see California. After we got a hitch-hiking ticket from a Texas state Trooper, another school chum who was going to California pulled over. We piled in and California here we come! Butch's girlfriend put us up at a friend's house in the hills of Laurel Canyon. This was the boom of the California Country Rock music scene and it was a fun week. We were lean on cash, so the mode of transport was thumb. Did I mention Butch's girlfriends name was Gidget? Not kidding.

One afternoon Gidget, Butch and I got picked up by a Mexican taxi driver on the strip who animatedly introduced himself as Manny. We tried to convince him we had no money and he assured us that was no problem and to get in. He was a happy guy. I had a bad feeling but went anyway. We were cruising around LA and our gregarious host was pointing out landmarks, telling us about himself and asking about us, where we were from, what we were doing in California etc.

We pulled up in front of a small cafe in a part of town that raised my hackles. We told him again that we had no cash. His personality was winning us over and into the cafe we went. He entered the room with a flair. Everyone seemed to know him. We took seats at a table as Manny kept a running commentary going. We were nineteen and I'm guessing the other patrons were in their thirties or forties, a pretty solid clientele for that time of day. A bottle of wine showed up on our table. We reiterated…. emphatically…. we had no money! He waved us off. Everyone was laughing and having fun and we got caught up in the party. Burritos, chimichangas and tacos arrived with the next bottle of wine. We were toasting, eating, singing and, I think, even dancing.

Cigars followed the next bottle of wine. Butch, Gidget and I were smoking cigars and the three of us were starting to look for a back-door escape. Our group was the obvious center of attention. Manny made sure of that. Maybe it was the wine, but everything seemed cool. As Butch and Gidget were dancing, I got close to Manny and explained once again that this was fun and we really enjoyed his company and appreciated the afternoon we were experiencing but we had no way to help out with the bill that was undoubtedly coming. He gestured for me to come closer, got a serious look on his face and said. "Have you ever heard the expression, Mi casa, su casa?" I said I hadn't.

He said, getting closer, "It means my house is your house." I looked around and realized there would be no check coming. I was a little embarrassed. Manny got up, did a quick spin with Gidget, directed us toward the door and with good wishes all around proceeded to take us to our original destination. No charge. Manny, it seemed, was just a good soul.

I've heard, and on many occasions invoked myself, the Manny mantra of "Mi casa, su casa.,"and when I do I'm always transported back to that afternoon in a small Hollywood cafe with Gidget, Butch and Manny. What were the arrangements with the proprietors of the cafe? Free taxi rides? Good will? I'll never know. But with hope in humanity restored Butch and I serendipitously (There's that word again.) landed jobs as gardeners and in a few days earned enough to fly back to El Paso on Academy Award night. A friend of Gidget's, who had a seat at the awards ceremony, took the time to drive us to the airport. Lessons learned. I thought back to that afternoon and the suspicious feeling, right or wrong, left. For good.

6

I was wide awake after my close encounter with the ET video chat and felt like an adventure. I outfitted myself in a flattering green wetsuit, hoped the atmosphere doodad adjusted to earth parameters and decided to explore. I waved at the door and after a few attempts it whooshed open or maybe just faded, I'm not sure which and I won't try to explain. I'll just relay to you what I was experiencing and maybe you'll have some thoughts. I sure hoped a summit could come together after this because there would be questions. I was still of the "throw enough at me and see what sticks" school. Between what stuck and my iPad scribblings I had a substantial overview.

I said out loud, "Lead me to the observatory." Immediately small lights on the floor lit at ten-foot intervals and guided my way. I assumed something would happen, and it did. I was getting spoiled. Two lefts, a right and a quick ride on the intergalactic elevator and I arrived at, I guess, the observatory. I stepped off and directly in front of me was the outline of a large door. A close cousin of the Egyptian hieroglyph was on the door. I waved at it and it physically vanished. I stepped through and what a sight.

The entire other end of the room, floor to ceiling, was a window to the outside universe. It was not a large room but had the size and appearance of a good-sized library reference room. Eight or nine tables and chairs were in rows. The tables each had ten chairs. One at each end and four on each side. It felt like a place of study or contemplation. There were bookcases stacked with the intergalactic iPad and........ books! I thought the room was empty but just behind me to my right was a gentleman staring at me with a look of jaw dropping wonder. So, I thought with way too much self-importance, you've heard of me. "Yes, I have," came the reply. I gotta watch that thinking thing or learn how the Aldairans edit. I walked over and introduced myself. He stood up and with that perfect British accent introduced himself as Drama and stuck out his hand. I took it and we shook hands mano a mano. Drama. That'd be a cool rap name. It was also the first name I'd heard that I could pronounce. That was good because Drama didn't look like anyone I knew. No nickname for him. He asked if I was feeling alright and I wasn't. He reached over and adjusted the knob/button/thingamajig on my suit and almost instantly I felt better.

"Thank you, Drama," I said. I was already overusing the cool rap name. The value of a bangin' nickname cannot be overemphasized. I played with a band some years back and wound up with the moniker "Spud." I think I ordered a baked potato at a diner one-night post gig, but I don't really remember. I was never crazy about Ted so I went with it. This crew was hanging and playing mainly in the North Jersey area so for now I was Spud and introduced myself as such. People reacted differently. "Hey Spud." How ya doin', Spud." Buy you a beer, Spud?" It would get overused. The name followed me to my next couple of bands and groups of acquaintances and so it went. It eventually faded out but to this day pops up every now and then. Linda has a grandson named Jake. He's going to be a popular kid.

So, this was Drama. ("How ya doin', Drama?" Buy you a beer, Drama?") He said he was hoping to meet me. He immediately asked what was our fascination with music and entertainment? It almost sounded rude, but this was just a universal cousin being curious. He'd been reading a book. The cover had the Aldairan hieroglyphics with a picture of a harp. Not the blues harp but the Harpo Marx sit down harp. I had an opportunity to play with a harpist at an afternoon summertime bash and it's a wonderful sounding instrument. It is not easy to play. Was Drama an aspiring musician? The thought popped into my head that except for the music of the universe I'd encountered earlier I hadn't heard any music since I left home. Home. I asked Drama how old he was, and he thought for a moment. "Thirty-seven earth years, "he said. I was stunned. He looked about sixteen. A quick lesson in Aldair's slightly smaller size, shorter days and quicker trip around their sun in relation to earth would put him at roughly eighteen or so in Aldair years. He told me Aldairans had a quality life span of about one hundred and forty earth years. Once the quality of life diminishes, they have the choice to move on. "To where," I said.

He thought to me, "You'll soon find out." Rather than sounding sinister it sounded like, man, was this going to be fun!

I explained to Drama about the overbearing extent of our emotions and how deeply music can affect us. I asked where his "emotional state" was and he said about thirty percent. I pulled out the well-worn life reflections and told him how I could hear "Red Rubber Ball" and I was back at a Piscataway High School dance or hit a game winning home run and feel like I was floating around the bases, or watch "Old

Yeller" and be reduced to tears. Music, movies, sports, Broadway and entertainment of all kinds are not only a part of humankind but in many ways define who we are. I was playing at a local bar about fifteen years ago and when I first walked in, I spotted a guy who turned out to be the owner wearing a Boston Red Sox cap. I had my Yankees cap on. We both took it in good humor and circled each other on the dance floor like a pair of pumas ready to rumble. That passed, we became pals and I reluctantly texted him congratulations when the Sox won the World Series. Finally.

I explained, "We are an emotional people. We put a lot of stock into "gut" feelings." Empires have risen and fallen on the back of emotion. I give you Marc Antony and Cleopatra, Romeo and Juliet, Bogie and Bacall. And don't forget Emperor Nero who, the story goes, decided to break out his fiddle as his Rome burned around him, or the Titanic quartet who opted to play to the bitter end rather than try to save themselves. Superman gave up his superpowers for the love of Lois Lane. Fortunately, he got them back in an interesting twist. I wasn't sure how much of that Drama got. The Superman reference was sure to soar over his head, but I threw it at him anyway.

"You are an interesting people, he said. "I hope you don't annihilate yourselves." This was said with no malice just very matter of factly.

"As do I, Drama" I replied.

He said, "Let's talk again," got up, shook my hand and whooshed out. I was left alone with a lot of questions as was my norm lately. Closer to the far window were some earthy looking chairs. I sat. Nothing moved or adjusted. It was just a comfortable chair. I pondered Aldair and the universe.

7

My thoughts turned once again to home. I guess I was going on about four days gone. So, Linda was either up on a charge of suspicion of murder or having to use her wits to explain my disappearance. Or maybe she just came clean right away. I know she was worried. I was worried. I was worried, excited, tired, hungry and basically, just wired.

I heard a whoosh and Sam walked in. He sat down and didn't say a word. He just looked down at Aldair.

After a minute he pointed and said, "That's my home, at the bottom right of that continent, the blue part that juts out." He said he hadn't been back in a month. It was considerate, I thought, of everyone to speak to me in Earth terms, Earth impressions. I didn't have to think so much. I asked him how old he was, and he said sixty, converting it to Earth terms. He looked thirty. He walked over to what I guessed was the magic food machine and produced something for himself. He brought back two slices of pizza and a coke for me. I hadn't had a coke in years, but I didn't want to be rude. I thanked him and we ate. The coke tasted nothing like coke but the pizza may have been the best I ever had. Why could they nail one and not the other?

I told him I'd met and had an interesting conversation with Drama. That was met with a look of confusion and a smile. He said something. I assume it was the correct pronunciation of Drama's name. He'll always be Drama to me. He asked if I had any children and I gave the typical macho answer, "No, at least, none that I know of." Wink!

The older I get the creepier that sounds. Sam told me he had seven children. I had questions. He followed up with, "There's no physical interaction, just science." That answers that. "And within your own race," I asked? He replied in the affirmative. That was going to be a hard sell.

8

I had a wake-up moment in 1969, my junior year at Piscataway High School. The times they were, and had been, a changin' for a while now. We moved from

Plainfield to Piscataway in 1965 at the height of racial unrest and the Plainfield/Newark riots. Once I heard shooting in my backyard, I told my mother I was now on board with the moving thing. I was in my first band and had my first girlfriend but as the last of two white guys left in the neighborhood, Stanley being the other one, and not much help, I was ready for greener and less painful pastures.

So, on a warm morning in the spring of 1969 the Piscataway High school student body was called to an assembly, always a good excuse to get out of class. The Black Renaissance Club was going to show what they were all about. I honestly wasn't all that interested, but it got me out of class. The auditorium was packed as the lights went down. From the rear came two lines of boys and girls in black robes holding candles and singing We Shall Overcome. So far, about what I expected. The crowd was polite, curious and maybe a little confused. As the members of The Black Renaissance Club approached and ascended the stage my epiphany started to take shape.

I didn't expect to see any white faces on the stage but there they were. Joining, or trying to join, the Black Renaissance club hadn't even been on my radar. I assumed you had to be black! The fifteen or twenty white faces jumped out at me from the stage as did something else. The white faces belonged to all the "smart kids," the chess club and AV guys. I was comfortable traveling within and around the different social groups, jocks, geeks, etc. They were the groups who would come out to see my band on weekends. And there they were on stage, the smart kids, as members of the Black Renaissance Club. Did they know something I didn't? They did. I wasn't sure what it was, but I was feeling small. I don't remember if they took any heat for their participation but if they did it didn't seem to stop them. The Black Renaissance Club continued until I graduated and beyond.

Linda and I just saw The Green Book in one of our rare ventures out to the movies. The Green Book was the bible for African Americans traveling through the south in the fifties and sixties and probably earlier and maybe even later. It was a directory to restaurants, hotels etc. where African Americans of the day could eat and stay in relative safety. The movie centers on the relationship between a white man and a black man. The white guy is hired to drive the black guy, a NY doctor and stellar piano player, as he performs a series of concerts with his trio. Tony was a "peacekeeper" at the Copacabana and his talents are put to use as the tour takes them though the south of the 1960's. Tony is and isn't a racist. He's a product of the Bronx of the day. Driver and client learn from each other.

Tony, his family, the Black Renaissance Club, the kids from the north who went down south for the freedom rides, some to never return, the black kids who sat at the southern soda fountains and endured repeated beatings were all operating on a different wavelength than a lot of the rest of us. They got it. The racial divide, as far as reproduction, worked for the Aldairans. They reached a level of acceptance without bigotry. Viva la difference. Welcome without judging. What would NYC be without Little Italy, Chinatown, Harlem or Hell's kitchen"? Boring!

The skin tone of the Aldairans is the same planet wide, as far as I can tell. Although with the return of emotions they see a slight return to a variety of pigmentation. As I told them, I'd relay the message but these days even the messenger suffers slings and arrows. Bring it.

9

I was back in my room. Sam went his own way. I was waiting for a "Let's hit the road" message to be followed by a meeting in the docking area. I guess the galactic Siri will lead me there. I used what little time I had to write, write and write. I also ordered a chocolate milk shake from the food god and it vibrated into existence. Not bad.

I was excited and nervous. In a little while I'd be on an alien planet, in an alien solar system interacting with an alien civilization. I was relieved that Dr Benjamin Franklin and who knows how many others paved the way. I wouldn't be looked at like a complete freak. But I hoped I could bring something to the party. In the field of science, technology and astrophysics I got nothin'. I was eyes wide open in that regard.

As far as emotion, feelings, appreciation of the arts within my limited knowledge and the game of love, also within my limited knowledge, I'd have a captive audience. I should have had a chat with Dr. Ben on how far he'd taken these subjects and were the Aldairans even that interested. I wondered if I could possibly talk Benjamin Franklin into coming Earth side with me, if only for a while.

I was getting a strange feeling that the Aldairans were pulling back from real first contact with us and were more interested in just letting us know that we're not alone, that we have brothers and sisters out there and could we please focus on living the Golden Rule. I hoped they'd at least give us the skinny on the intergalactic food machine. The hamburger needs work, but the pizza was out of this world. Sam's face appeared on the wall screen. We'd be leaving shortly.

Part 6

**

1

I was glad Sam was my first contact. He gave off a host/big brother/cool kind of vibe and I was comfortable around him. It was him and me in the egg traveling toward his home on Aldair. It felt like two guys on a road trip. You know those trips. You're sitting around a kitchen table at one thirty in the morning and someone says, "Let's go to Florida." Nine hours later you're approaching North Carolina, hung over and wondering what the hell you got yourselves into. And there's no going back. Who's gonna be the one to be the grownup and say, "Ya know what, I think we made a mistake. Let's go back." No one!

I think Sam looked happy, even excited. We were in our familiar egg and I was anticipating the next adventure with my space pal. We were at cruising speed and seemed to be lazily working our way down. Mother egg had disappeared, but the Mother ship was still visible, barely.

I'd showered, eaten, slept, emptied myself in every manner and was ready to rock. My focus was directly here, and I figured I'd get home when I got home. Sam kicked it into overdrive, and we made a beeline drop toward a large, large body of water. Once again, we did that drop in, slow down and slightly pull up maneuver. We were about twenty feet above water that was a beautiful familiar green tropical color. It wasn't the blue or blue green Bermuda /Bahama color but a darker green that maybe I'd seen in pictures or movies. It was very calm with small rolling waves. I couldn't see land. The sky was a glorious light blue and there wasn't a cloud in sight. The sun, a brilliant orange ball, seemed larger than ours, maybe a matter of proximity, and low in the sky. Sunrise? Sunset? We were both standing, and Dave looked like he was just having fun, like a kid on a jet ski. I asked if the atmosphere was ok for me. He tweaked my gizmo and "cracked a window."

I smelled mother ocean. My old pal Bruce, my Piscataway neighbor who'd joined me in El Paso, would cite the ocean as his personal cure all. If he had a cold, flu, poison ivy or any myriad of ailments his mantra would be "If I could just get to Mother Ocean." I must admit I've used mother ocean as my family doctor on more than one occasion. It was certainly a cure all on a Sunday morning after a Beach Haven Saturday night.

We were hauling across the top of the waves even catching spray on the outside of the egg. And shut my mouth if a school of something resembling dolphins wasn't keeping up. With the opening in the egg I could hear the chattering of the fish (mammals?) I was getting sprayed, by what I wasn't sure, but it smelled and tasted like mother ocean. Man, this was a glorious moment. Sam was enjoying watching me having a thrill and damned if he wasn't sporting a huge smile. He made a fast arcing u turn and our companions followed us. There were hundreds of them breaking water, chattering, running into each other and coming so close I could smell them. I don't know what else to call them but dolphins. That's what they were. Sam rose to about ten feet and stopped. Our friends were all around us, some doing that backward tail walking thing. I had an urge.

"Is it safe?" I asked. Sam was on board. He led me to where the opening was and pushed me out! No helmet. I had a quick thought and hoped this wasn't the reason I was here. (The earthlings are a wonderful, nutritious source of protein for our sea life.) I refer you to The Twilight Zone, "To serve man.... it's a cookbook!" Too late. I was submerged and the water was almost too warm, like a bath. The creatures were all around, coming close but not touching. I dove down a few feet. and paddled around. It was an abyss below me. I came up and hung out with my new pals. They seemed to enjoy my company. There was a splash next to me. I guess it's not dinner unless Sam was also on the menu, too. He disappeared and stayed disappeared. Should I be worried? He came up after about a minute and had something in his hand. It looked like a small turtle with no shell. He showed it to me and sent it on its way.

I was petting the dolphin closest to me and its skin was like satin. It didn't seem to mind. Sam motioned time to go. The egg was right on top of the water. Sam grabbed two handles that appeared on each side and pulled himself in. I followed. Our suits were immediately dry. He handed me a towel and I did a quick hair face dry off but not too much. It felt good. Mother ocean. Wow!

I mentioned to Sam that the dolphins looked like...... dolphins. He said I shouldn't be surprised. They came from earth. A group of them were brought from earth two hundred and fifty years ago and were flourishing in the thinner nutrient rich water of Aldair. Should I be miffed that they absconded with our friendly little dolphins, our sea puppies? They certainly seemed happy. And how many generations along were they at this point, anyway? He added that the consensus was they were originally brought to Earth from who knows where. It seems dolphins are also adaptable creatures. Except for the "different" looking lady I had run into on the ship earlier I was getting the impression that maybe the universe really was more similar than we can imagine. Sam must have read me and said there were many similarities in many places, but varieties also abound. Earth like planets produce earthly cousins. But there are many planets not at all like Earth or Aldair. That's an interesting way to put it, I thought. He said my trip would be limited but hoped I'd continue to find it interesting. Sam was the king of understated understatement. I was still in watch and absorb mode. I hoped an earthly round table Q and A was in my future. I had to unload a barrel full of questions soon.

Before I could reply to the dolphin revelation Sam gunned it and we were ripping across the water leaving the fishy grandchildren behind. They followed as long as they could. We pulled up to about twenty feet and in the distance coming into view were cliffs.

Between us and the cliffs was something I can only describe as a replica of a Hollywood version portal. If the director came to the special effects guys and said a portal was needed, this is what they'd get. It was a circular one hundred feet tall, glowing entrance...or exit to...where? All that was visible was a thin red circular outline and a golden shimmering interior. We slowed, I guess, so I could have a better look. Every ten seconds or so a vehicle or person or group of vehicles or persons would enter or exit, somehow knowing enough not to smash into each other.

Sam said, "Yes. It's a portal, to many, many destinations." 'Nuff said.

Sam gunned it and we were heading toward shore, toward the cliffs. They looked like the White Cliffs of Dover but dark, dark brown, almost black. The tall dark cliffs jumped out against the green water and blue sky. Picture the California cliffs along the Pacific Coast Highway, only higher, darker and smoother. We were on top of them quickly. Maybe Sam had to behave himself in front of his peers, but here he was a hotshot. I still didn't know what he was, if he and his crew were scientists, astronauts, some kind of military or maybe an expeditionary team. Another query. We were getting close. I wasn't going to say anything. He looked over at me and I just looked ahead, grinning. He pulled up, fast. Sam touched something and my balance was neutralized. We were climbing almost straight up the cliffs. And then over. And there it was. My first glimpse of an "other worldly" city. Meet George Jetson!

The city was about nine or ten miles away but clearly visible past a field of impressive flowers that went on as far as I could see on either side and ended in a stretch of green as meticulously kept as any golf course putting green. The flowers were of all shapes and sizes, some alone, some in groups, some very bushy and some looking very delicate. We were just over the ground and I could see patches of green wherever there was space. We're comin' in. Wait'll they get a load of me!

2

It looked like we were headed to a massive group of airline terminals. Each "terminal" consisted of a large central circular area the size of a small town with spokes coming out in every direction. The spoke configuration seemed to be an Aldaiaran constant, ala the Mother Ships docking areas. It seemed to make ergonomic sense. Attached to the bottom of each spoke on either side and at regular intervals running the entire length of the spoke were what resembled round coffee or soup mugs. It was as if the spoke was a street and the mugs were houses on either side of the street. The whole group was a stunning white marble color and geometrically perfect. Between the rug of gorgeous flowers and the brilliance of the scene before me I was at a loss for words. I guess I had a few thoughts as Sam was looking at me with that weird, "Waddaya think of that" grin. As we got closer, I could see two thin wires attached from the main circular area to the end of each spoke. The "wires" emitted a glow and a soft hum that I couldn't see or hear but felt was there, nonetheless. No explanation. The terminal was situated on four large posts each one having windows and an opening at ground level.

We carried on until we were cruising the street between the cups. Each spoke was about four hundred yards long (I think in terms of football fields) and the street was about fifty yards wide. The cups had windows and doors and were obviously residences, covering the area above and below the walkway. All in all, a cool, clean look. There was a walkway that went from the end of each spoke to the terminal and was accessible from each home, just outside a door. There were eggs of different sizes next to several doorways or on the side of the homes. The homes were close, maybe fifteen yards apart. There was a slightly different hieroglyph on each. Numbers? Addresses? About a third of the way down Sam made a right and we stopped outside what I guessed was Sam's place. Each home had individual walkways; one going to a front door and one going to a side door. We "parked" at the side door and Sam shut her down. Home sweet home.

2

Sam's interstellar bachelor pad was a very earthy looking kind of home. Everything was done with voice commands in the Aldairan language. It was a smooth sound that I still could make no sense of. There was apparently an Alexa type device running the joint. Sam's place was Spartan. There were chairs, tables, a couch, bedroom and an obvious kitchen. Sam looked like he was talking to the wall, but a screen had appeared, and he was talking to Dave. Dave gave me a wave and welcomed me to Aldair.

I remembered Sam had mentioned a family, but the Aldairan family dynamic was sure to be foreign to me. In good time. Dave said he'd see me at the center, my interpretation, and signed off. Sam said he needed rest. I asked him if it was ok for me to walk around and he said remember where his home was and something akin to don't get into any trouble. He assured me no one would be too surprised by my appearance, but I might be an object of curiosity. Maybe I'd just hang out. He pointed out the intergalactic food machine and then asked if I'd like an Aldairan history lesson. Indeed, I would. He spoke to the wall and a video/hologram of Aldairan history commenced. He said say pause, end, go back etc. and it would understand. What was "it?"

For the next forty five minutes or so I enjoyed a slice of pizza, as good as the one I had earlier and a cold glass of water, along with a holographical Aldairan history lesson in clear English with, of course, a British accent. I learned that they were us. Unless there's some strange genetic turn, we all look similar and develop along the same learning curve. Somehow, they managed to stop killing each other much earlier on than we did and opted to work together for a better, stronger Aldair. I have to think their lack of emotions may have had something to do with that, rational thinking with no ulterior motive other than making your home the best it can be. It could also explain their interest in but lack of production, seemingly, of music, plays and the arts in general. A good love song needs emotion, plenty of it, as does a play, book or movie intended to move and convince someone else that they could be the next one to do that. To quote Miami Steve Van Zandt," We knew we couldn't be the Beatles. But then the Stones came along. We could do that!"

I learned that not all races got the "Can't we all get along," philosophy. Not all species learn that lesson. Some destroy themselves, some cripple themselves for generations and some come out for the better on the other side. The Aldairans came out better earlier on the other side and they hold out hope that we can do the same. Well I guess we have come a long way since the Inquisition, although man's inhumanity to man still prevails in pockets on our planet.

As far as developing towns and cities, modes of transportation, and early space explorations we were on a similar path. A monetary system disappeared shortly after their "enlightenment." There was just no need. Food and clothing were provided. Living space was provided and everyone was working toward becoming better Aldairans and furthering the nurturing of places like Earth. I don't know and never found out how the economics of that worked but it did. I guess if food, and in all likelihood, other needs are provided by asking the magic machine then the manpower cost is nonexistent. We're starting to tap into that idea with the 3 D copier. Exciting stuff. I kept waiting for the other shoe to drop but it wasn't dropping. Where did the ant person creature fit in? There was no mention in the hologram. I said stop and the wall resumed its…. wallness. I stepped outside and pulled a lounge chair out of the side of Sam's home. I mean right out of the side. It was somehow attached. I fell into solid comfort. The Aldairans seemed to enjoy their comfort. Once again, I passed out.

I woke up when I felt something licking my hand. It was a dog! Did I mention I love dogs? Something else they borrowed from us? He/she was a small mutty dog, my favorite kind, and had a friendly, intelligent look about it. Sam came out a minute later and the pup was all over him.

"Yours?" I asked and with a waving arc of his hand he said, "Ours."

I looked toward the end of Sam's walkway and saw that I was indeed a curiosity. Two kids akin to ten or twelve-year-old Earth kids could not take their eyes off me. I made a sudden move toward them and they jumped. I couldn't help it. Sam gave me a look. I laughed hopefully showing I was but a likeable good-natured lout and walked toward them with the doggie. I said hello and they looked surprised and slightly dumbfounded. Maybe they'd never heard the English language. I waved and left the dog with them. They waved back. I turned back to join Sam and he motioned me to the rear of his home. The walkway continued around and back out to the entry walkway which led up to the main walkway which led to the terminal. From the rear of his home I saw terminals and homes out to the horizon, all very generic.

Sam told me that each terminal or group of terminals is devoted to a specific area, exploration within their star system, further out exploration, botany, health, education etc, some overlapping and mixing and matching. I asked if there was any criminal activity or prisons of any kind, a human question. Sam said, "No." The children had left, and it was getting dark. Sam asked if I'd mind being left alone overnight. He wanted to visit his mate and children. I was a little hurt. How 'bout me? He said he'd like them to meet me before we left.

"At your convenience," I said. He took my hand, looked directly into my eyes and said, "Thank you." I think we had a moment. He was also a likable, good-natured lout. Wow. A night alone on a distant planet in another star system. I would never have pictured this a week ago, in my wildest dreams, and I have wild dreams.

Sam went in and I, once again, felt extremely far away from home, and a little homesick. Every now and then I'd see an egg in the distance or a mother egg or two lazily, or not so lazily, floating by. It was getting dark very slowly and I remembered that Aldair was one and a half times the size of Earth. That must make for an extended sunrise and sunset experience. Did they appreciate that experience as much as we do, enough to write songs about them? I hoped so. I was gonna get a beer and take up a seat for my first Aldairan sunset. Sam came out and showed me how to get in and out of his home. He answered my unasked question about the need to lock up. No need. "I'll be back shortly after sunup," he said. I was looking forward to some alone, looking around time. I said, "Have fun storming the castle." Not a Monty Python fan? He checked my oxygen regulator and advised me not to adjust it or remove my suit till tomorrow. He said he was surprised at my self-sufficiency. I think that's what he said. I was surveying the brilliant green carpet below. There were people here and there walking. When I turned around Sam was gone.

I went in and got a cold beer. I think I said chilled and it was frosty. I opened the wall video and started to continue with the Aldairan history. They'd colonized two planets in their solar system and one of their two moons. In addition, five other moons were used in one manner or another, originally to spread out. That was their first foray into their space, the idea being getting ahead of the overcrowding curve. I always assumed that overcrowding would become one of Earth's prime dilemmas in the coming decades. I had read an article that put forth the notion that population growth was slowing and at some point, would reach an equilibrium of sorts. I forget the nuts and bolts of the argument, but I remember it made sense. The Aldairans had reached that equilibrium before population growth became a life-threatening issue. Their washed-out emotional state led to a more pragmatic, for them, population control paradigm. By the time they experience a full emotional jump start, they'll have solved the potential problem. They went all in on their space race as they jumped across their system and the galaxy. This tiny section of it was their home. They left the ant guy's moon alone and really didn't seem to have much to do with them. That race had settled there as they jumped across the cosmos. The ants seemed to have a friendly working relationship with the Aldairans and not much more. I couldn't figure out how I was able to understand the language of the video, but I did. It was coming to me as pictures and impressions, like everything else. I got a slice of pizza and another beer and headed outside. There was a lush islands kind of feeling with perfumed air permeating everything. It was much darker now, and the blanket of green seemed to go on forever. That was it, terminals and the forever lawn, and surprise, lights way off in the distance. A city? I took up a spot in the lounger and started laughing. Too cosmic.

There was a large moon in the upper right nighttime sky that glowed a brilliant bluish white. It was a little over half full and felt close enough to reach out and touch. Way over to the left and lower was a second moon that was much smaller, also half full but very bright. It looked familiar. I spotted what

I thought were planets in two other places, too large for stars at this range and too small for moons. They looked to be about three times the size of the morning Venus on earth.

Maybe it was the two beers or the combination of the rich air and lounger but the next thing I felt was the sun on the back of my neck. The pale blue sky of yesterday was replaced by a dark indigo sky and large blue white clouds. The moons were gone, and eggs were zipping by at regular intervals. Rush hour? Two were hovering about twenty feet out. The occupants seemed to be having a conversation. Maybe I was being paranoid, but they were looking at me? I should do something earthy. I've been known to break into dance at the drop of a hat. Here goes. I got up and they disappeared. I thought I saw a wave. I went in and ordered one of my breakfast staples, Raisin Bran with a cut up banana. It was close. Some orange juice and a cup of toe-curling coffee and I was ready to roll. I walked out to the end of the walkway at the opposite end of the terminal. There was a kind of hanging out area with a few tables and chairs and, yes, tiki lamps.

I passed several people on the way out and got friendly nods and a few of those strange handshakes, but no conversation. Maybe that was a special talent that Sam and Dave were tuned in to. As per Sam's explanation this was the terminal primarily dedicated to exploration and related endeavors. So, seeing an alien visitor, me, was probably not unusual. The homes continued below the walkway. My first impression of the "cups" hanging below was being adjusted. The cup area seemed to be another living area or possibly a garage. On my level was a bubble type enclosure that was the main living area. Very economic, interesting and clean. No obvious wasted space.

It was getting warm as the sun rose, warmer than yesterday. I returned to Sam's, had another cup of coffee, specifying not too strong and opened the video screen. I was shouting commands; "sports, news, cartoons," but nothing was happening. If I said play, more Aldairan history started right where I'd left off. I guess Sam took the flipper. I dug out the ipad and continued my notes.

3

"We are stardust. We are golden. We are billion-year-old carbon. And we've got to get ourselves back to the garden." That's Joni Mitchell and I believe she nailed it. I wondered if this was the way it went throughout the galaxies. Some ancient Johnny Appleseed sprinkling stardust and hoping for the best. Theories abound; the aforementioned universe in the shoe of a giant, the biblical God, a computer simulation, dimensions, timelines crossing or maybe just a peculiar dream.

How about this? God created an intricate computer simulation, gave a giant a home in a "Garden of Eden" within it, inserted our universe in the heel of his shoe, then created multiple universe simulations and that's His/Her Saturday night TV entertainment. Maybe He/She tunes into prayers and throws us a helping hand now and then. Maybe not. Maybe, like us, God enjoys watching people fall into the cake at weddings or skateboarders slipping off a railing and doing a face plant. My question has always been how a loving God can allow the earthly sufferings. There really is no answer. As the nuns would say, "Well, it's a mystery." The catch all. I'd say be cool, don't hurt anyone and give it your best shot. If, along the way, you manage to make a diving catch of a blistering line drive, fall in love a few times, get to know a bunch of great dogs or cats, climb some trees, help out a few folks, eat an apple right off the branch, body surf a great wave and enjoy the pleasure of being here, well, I guess that's enough.

At the risk of repeating myself I keep returning to a lot of the same thoughts. Ant man notwithstanding, the thought is how similar we are. The Aldairan history "video" drove the point home. It makes sense. Whoever or wherever we are we start out with no skills and are merely trying to stay warm and comfortable. At the same time, we're trying to not get eaten by whatever may be trying to eat us and to keep our own bellies full.

I think the need for companionship must be universal. We eventually learn to communicate and live with each other and create tribes. Then we develop a way to travel so we can communicate with the guy down the road, then further and further down the road. We map our world and after staring up at the stars for thousands of years attempt to map and visit them. An "enlightenment" of some kind eventually occurs. Planets overpopulate or die out for any number of reasons, some natural, some a causation of cocky misbehaving. My words. Those that make it, really make it.

This is where the Aldairans are, taking baby steps across the Milky Way and letting folks know we're all in this together in their own quirky Aldairan way. I feel like we're starting our own "enlightenment." We're realizing that the earth won't last forever, and we'd better be nice to it. We're waking up to the fact that we're all brothers and sisters and we have to take care of and watch out for each other. Some get this, some don't. Our technology seems to be picking up steam. Just when I start to really feel comfortable with my iPhone the next one comes out. There also seems to be frivolous technological devices coming down the pike for no reason other than they can. The guys in the automobile labs have to earn their keep, as we all do. Thus, heated seats, rear and side view mirror cameras etc. and so on. But how quickly we adapt to these small changes and miss them when they're not there.

Some of these seemingly unimportant items are refined, developed further and adopted by the military or Nasa. Then one day we see someone on the International Space Station using something that we'd seen at a high school science fair five years earlier, a new and improved widget. One breakthrough leads to ten others.

In 1903 the Wright Brothers made their flight at Kitty Hawk. Sixty plus years later we were walking on the moon. Now we've got rovers on Mars, an international space station, a craft leaving our system and we're landing on comets! We don't even know the half of what's going on. We can find out but most times we're just waiting for the headline grabbers. There's a lot going on under the surface. Numerous experiments that may not be sexy but start a chain of discovery.

My job leads me into forty-five-minute conversations with the medical and pharmaceutical community, among others. Breakthroughs are here or on the horizon. They are a committed bunch and though we all complain about the cost of medications or treatments and the time it takes to get a drug into the mainstream, I can tell you, they're trying, and succeeding, particularly in the battle against cancers. I can only guess where we'll be in one hundred or five hundred years. Exponential.

A massive flock of birds flew by overhead. They looked like Cardinals but much larger, the size of a hawk. Three kids, or small adults, were weaving in and around and over and under the flock eliciting loud squawks from the birds. The kids seemed to be free flying with no obvious means of propulsion. Did I mention everyone I've seen was wearing the wetsuit uniform with the various designations in the upper right chest area? They made a diversion down to my area and hung there staring. I saw they had small controls in their hands but what they were controlling was not obvious. They checked me out for a minute and gave, I think, a quick acknowledgment and buzzed off to continue harassing the birds. Looked like fun.

4

I thought I remembered Sam had said their enlightenment was eight hundred years ago. I'd pictured our earth of five hundred years in the future to be more futuristic. I was standing at the edge of

Sam's deck when I looked down and saw that the egg was there. It seemed to be the same one we'd been using. I also noticed once again how gorgeously green and well-kept the ground was, as far as I could see. Terminals and grass. The city I'd seen last night was no longer visible. More questions.

I heard a soft whirring sound and Sam landed right next to me in a small flying saucer. That's what it was, a flying saucer, a two-seater. It seemed to be locked in place a few inches off the edge of the deck, the way the iPad was able to be locked in place in air on the egg. How'd they do that? Sam simply stepped out of his craft and onto the deck much like stepping off a boat onto a dock. I wondered how he'd gotten to where he was coming from if our egg was still here.

"How was your evening," he asked?

"Contemplative," I thought. He got it. We went inside and Sam had some food while I continued the iPad. He told me he'd had a wonderful visit with his family and some acquaintances. I asked him if he could be in love with his mate if they had little or no emotions. He said they were coming back in varying degrees. Why it was different from one person to another he couldn't say but he seemed very sensitive to it and felt an affection for his wife. She didn't feel quite that but cared for and respected him very much. I asked if she lived in the city I'd seen last night. He looked at me kind of quizzically and said no. But there was a place he thought I'd be very keen to see.

"Are you interested in your history?" he asked.

I replied, "Yes, very much."

"Would you like to see your history?" he asked, and let it hang there. What did that mean I wondered? That strange "I know something you don't" grin came out once again.

He led me over to an area at the end of the wall and an indentation appeared. It looked a lot like the Mother Ship elevator. He grabbed a plate, placed it in the wall dent, touched some invisible buttons and the plate did a wavy, humming disappearing act.

Sam said, "To your earlier question, that's how I prefer to get around. (grin) I asked if that was a disassembling and reassembling of molecules and he said no. It was another mode of travel. To quote The Temptations I was a "Ball of Confusion," but still willing to be led along this strange, once in a lifetime path.

I thought about New Jersey and wondered how things were going when a bang startled both of us. One of those large birds had flown into a window on the other side of the room. It seemed a little stunned then flew off. Sam gave a command to the room and I could feel something happen around the window. He apologized and said that shouldn't happen again. He went out and checked the sky. An equivalent of a thumbs up followed. I guess the bird was ok. He went into the other room. I hadn't looked around, but I guess it was a bedroom. The bathroom, which I had found, was adjacent to this main room. Sam came out and handed me another wetsuit. He said he'd be busy for a while so carry on. I went outside, pulled up a chair and got back to writing. I could hear some chatter from inside. I couldn't eavesdrop if I wanted to, just waited for the next adventure.

5

Sam woke me a short time later. I slept pretty well in my own bed, but this was on another level. Sam said the chair can sense your physical and mental state and helps put you to sleep. Now that's a new one. He said it can be controlled and he should have mentioned that. It looked like we were ready to go. I swapped suits and ordered some fried chicken from the galactic chef. It was cold and not very good. I guess the chef was hit and miss. I wanted to continue as the civil guest, so I didn't mention that the chicken tasted like fish. But the water was cold and very tasty. A trip to the head and we were off.

I started to walk outside but Sam motioned me over to the "dishwasher." Once again came the cryptic, "Ready?" I followed Sam as he stepped into the wall indent which seemed to conform to whatever was placed in it. This time it was us. A control pad appeared in front of Sam's raised hand. I couldn't tell if it was on the wall or in the air. The room in front of my eyes was fading, like the elevator on the Mother Ship. I got it. The conveyance wasn't moving. We were. There was a sensation of almost passing out and then a different room materialized in front of us. Put one of these on my Christmas list. We stepped out into a large mall like area. I felt like I was in an actual NJ mall. There were a number of slightly inclined, slow moving, rug like escalators, two fountains, and what appeared to be stores. They weren't stores. It wasn't overcrowded but lots of folks were gathered here and there and moving in and out of the "stores." There were Aldairans of all sizes, a number of the "ant people," a few, what we would call "little people" but obviously not Aldairan little people. They were humanoid but not human, or Aldairan. And, shut my mouth, earthlings! I didn't know what the Aldairan terminology was for us so I deferred to the 1950's sci fi moniker. I started to walk toward them and was directed in another direction.

Sam said," They're not from your time." Their clothes were odd but what did not from your time mean? Our past? Our future? Sam, having "heard" me, stopped, looked me directly in the eye and said very clearly, "There is no past. There is no future. It's all happening right now." This seemed like something he really wanted me to understand. Of course, I couldn't. Like everything else I'd seen I got the concept, but the deep dive was way above my pay scale.

I've read a number of the life beyond the grave adventures, heaven, hell and other bizarre anomalies and always believed that there must be something after this. Otherwise, what's the point? The people that return from near death experiences have similar stories about time, or lack of it. Just recently I was reading an article that appeared on my Facebook page detailing this very notion. All is now. Time isn't a line but more of a circle. Again, the concept is about as far as I can go.

We started to walk in a different direction but not before I got a smile and a wave from a tall woman who was holding hands with another tall woman who both looked like they could have stepped off a bus in Hoboken. I'm sure I had a dumbfounded look on my face as I waved back. They looked at each other and laughed. It was good to see laughter. I laughed. Sam looked at me and we continued walking toward an escalator. We stepped onto something. It wasn't stairs but we were ascending. I was just about to step off at the top when it continued and more reality appeared around us. That's about the only way I can describe it. We came to another level. I just waited. Sam stepped off and I followed. For a moment I saw that the escalator went up and down to as many levels as I could see but then coalesced right here. Confusing? You bet.

We were in a much more severe looking area. There was a large picture window at one end of the large room otherwise, nothing. Markings on the wall every twenty feet or so, which had an Aldairan look to them, gave the only hint that something was there. Sam gave me that "How 'bout that" look again and I attempted my "Oh yeah, that was pretty cool, too" look. I was well into mental overload at this point and if a herd of pink elephants flew by, well, another day in this strange dream. A while back I was sitting at a light at the corner of Sixth Ave and Forty Eighth St, NYC. I was watching a guy walk a camel down the street. I snapped a pic and posted it on Facebook with the caption "Just another day in the big city." That was no dream, just a New York reality. Was this a dream? It didn't have any of the properties of a dream. And it went on way too long and in too much of a coherent manner if anything about this could have been called coherent. There was no one around as we approached one of the hieroglyphs and of course a door/entrance materialized, and we walked through.

Between the wonderful sleep I was getting and the rich atmosphere I'd been breathing I felt more awake than I had in years. Chauffeuring, music and morning radio don't leave a whole lot of time for sleep. As I've gotten older, I cannot sleep like I used to, anyway. Back in the day I could do ten or twelve hours easy. Now six or seven, even on a Saturday or Sunday is the norm. Ah, youth.

In my El Paso college days I had a sleeping adventure. When Butch and I returned from our California spring break trip I kind of checked out. I put a blanket over my window and slept for a week. I got up to eat or hang with my pals but other than that I was gone. I never could figure out why I did that, but I'd seen other guys go down that road at one point or another. A rite of passage? I had some 'splainin' to do but my professors bought my story. I don't remember what my story was, but I guess it worked. I look back on some of the things I've done or been involved in and feel a pang of embarrassment. I had my own "enlightenment" around age forty-five. As my geometry teacher will attest, I'm a slow learner. I described some of my misgivings earlier and all you can really do is learn and move on. I am a sensitive human being, Pisces, and all that. I don't put a whole lot of stock in astrology but in a broad sense it seems to be accurate, at least in personality traits. My past transgressions, though not huge or especially important in the scheme of things, seem to affect me more now than they did then. I guess that's a good thing. There are mistakes I wouldn't make again. The lesson, I think, is own your past, all of it, no excuses and listen to that little voice in your head, that feeling in your belly that says, "Uh uh. Don't do it." We all have it. Mine's become more front and center and I'm glad of it.

7

Sam and I walked through one of the magic doors and entered an antiseptic feeling room, kind of like a doctor's office. There was a console and a young looking Aldairan man who was working intently on something. He looked up and with a smile and a look of amazement came around and warmly greeted me with an enthusiastic earthly handshake. Sam introduced him with another Aldairan name I couldn't quite understand. It sounded like Drury. Sam said Drury was younger and more emotionally evolved. Sam was a mentor of a sort to Drury, and others, as I'd come to see. He just had a warm manner about him. I asked Sam where we were and relating it to earth terms, he said we were in a terminal about one hundred and fifty miles from his home. That was a quick trip! He used the word terminal. He came close to me and said, "terminal?" I did a quick vamp about airline terminals with their main hub and "spokes" going out to the different gates, and how as we were coming in that's the first thought that popped into my head. Terminals. He got it. This terminal was an entertainment, get away, meeting and greeting kind of spot. Sam said, "Have fun, and learn," and left. Drury gave me that, "It's you and me, man" look. Interpreting looks is a talent I've always had.

He asked me if I could pick a segment of Earth history to visit what would that be. The all is now timeline, I thought. I didn't quite get what he was driving at. He said we can bring the past into this room, not a representation but the actual event. He said we can't interact or be seen but can be in the moment to observe, walk in and around but not affect in any way. My mind was righteously boggled. What an opportunity! What to do. Where to go. "I can do that now? Anywhere? Anytime?" I said.

"Yes", was the reply, delivered with a "let's get on with this adventure," chuckle. I liked this guy. He seemed very earthy. He looked to be about twenty and had an insignia on his wetsuit that I hadn't seen before. As I was contemplating this amazing opportunity Drury was patiently waiting for an answer. I had it.

8

Jesus Christ. That's not an exclamation. That's who I wanted to see. Did you ever see the Saturday Night Live cartoon starring the Man of the hour? It's rerun every Christmas and it's right on the mark. We have Jesus walking through Anytown, USA and he sees televangelist Pat Robertson on a TV in a store window. He's impressed because Pat is saying all the right things. Jesus hightails it down to the studio and excitedly tries to get on stage, but Pat just keeps talking and elbowing Him out of the way, not missing a beat. The hilarity is that the audio is real, and the animation is made to fit. Jesus is bummed and has the same outcome when he runs into Jerry Falwell and Robert Schuller. Lots of zealous religious talk but they just can't recognize Jesus. So, the Savior hits the streets again and stops outside a grammar school. The front door is open and there's a commotion inside. As it starts to snow, he realizes he's watching the Christmas story.......His Christmas story...... being played out by the Peanuts gang. His face brightens as Linus delivers a soliloquy about the true meaning of Christmas. Well, at the end Jesus just turns to the camera with a big grin on his face and breaks into the Snoopy dance accompanied by the Peanuts soundtrack. You know the tune.

I've mentioned that Catholicism was beaten into me for eight years by the Sisters of (no) Mercy. Since then I've come to learn that Jesus' message was simple. It wasn't a one-hundred-page catechism of rules. It was love your neighbor. Forgive and forget. Give the hungry guy a sandwich. Keep an eye on your own house and don't worry so much about anyone else's. Be cool. The Sisters didn't dwell on that. They liked to talk about how hot the fires of hell are.

I just finished a book about the historical Jesus. Not the prophet or the Son of God but the actual person who walked the earth some two thousand years ago, developed a following and was put to death by the Romans. Was he the Son of God or just a charismatic prophet who told people what they needed to hear? Either way He had a good message, but it sure put some people off. I wanted to see this. Would it really be possible? I told Drury I'd like to see Jesus in his heyday. He wasn't sure what I was talking about, so I filled him in and he got to work behind his console. Googling Jesus?

There was a mirror or reflective apparatus on the far wall. I looked very strange. I looked at Drury. He looked normal. They were a beautiful people. Us, at least me, not so much. He was decidedly Aldairan but with blonde hair and a slightly bronze complexion. His pigments were working overtime. He could have been an 1880's Native American who needed a little more time in the sun. He looked up, walked over and said that not only emotionally but physically his people were rebounding, and rebounding rapidly. Each generation was two steps further along than the next generation. He asked if I'd been told about the results of mixing races. I said I had, and I would pass it along but it would do no good. We love strongly. And we never know where or how it will strike. He understood.

"It will be an interesting future for Aldair," he said. He told me his mate was from the northern region of Aldair. She was pure white with jet black hair and he thought they were in love. That was an unusual conversation. I had some questions then he said, "Ready?" There's that feeling in my belly again. The good feeling.

9

Drury took his place back behind the console and instructed me to observe and move in and around all I wanted. No one would notice me. As his voice trailed off a mist or haze or fog was coming in from somewhere. And then.... bang! It was as if someone hit the on button and cranked up the volume. I was about one hundred yards from the bank of a large lake. There was a lot of action on the lake, small boats coming and going. I turned just as an old woman pointed and yelled something. I was about to get run over by a cart, but it went through me. I was in the middle of a dirt road and the woman was pointing at a group of people walking our way. I looked back and could just make out Drury. He was at his console but out of the picture, as it were. People were dressed in exactly what I expected, toga type garments of all colors. But some had what looked like loose Karate uniforms. I never saw that in the history books. It was hot. Extremely hot. I was there. Or they were here. I looked back at the approaching group. They'd stopped and were taking seats under a group of three trees. One man stood and walked to the far tree. He picked three pieces of fruit and tossed two to the group. A few outstretched hands and the fruit disappeared. Pears? They all laughed. A group of about twenty were coming up the road. I looked back at the man who picked the fruit. He was looking directly at me, through me. It was Jesus. He didn't look much like the picture that had hung in our dining room for years, but it was Jesus. He was a little shorter and stockier than we'd been led to believe. He was very middle eastern looking. But his dark brown hair, parted in the middle and hanging just below his ears, had bold blonde streaks. His Roman nose separated a long chin and large blue eyes. He looked strong and healthy. But why was he looking at me? A man walked past me and straight up to Jesus. He was speaking to Jesus in a language I'd never heard. Jesus had his hand on the man's shoulder as he pointed toward the river and gently guided the man away. Jesus was smiling. The man was weeping. It'd gone very quiet. Then gradually one person, then two, then three were talking and eating but with more excitement as if something special had just happened. The tree's roots spread out along the ground and Jesus sat. It became quiet again. Jesus spoke. What he was saying I don't know but his voice was the only sound in the heat of the afternoon. I moved up next to him. I sat next to him. He spoke softly but could be heard in the back of the crowd which now numbered about fifty. The sound of his voice was calming. I felt like I was understanding the message even though I couldn't. Could I? Was this like the Aldairan communication? Impressions?

I was starting to feel like I was intruding, but like I was a welcome intruder if that's possible. I stood up and walked to the back of the crowd then to the point where I'd come in. I could still hear Jesus clearly. I had a feeling that if I stayed much longer, I would never leave. A sadness came over me. I looked back at Jesus and noticed an older woman had moved up next to him. Her heart would soon be broken when she'd see her son murdered. I motioned to Drury that I'd had enough. The scene faded but I heard Jesus' voice for a second or two after the room was clear. I was confused.

I said to Drury, "Was that here? Was I there?"

" It was here, and you were there, he said. It's all happening now." I was getting a headache. Damn that Einstein! Drury was looking at me like I was supposed to say something. No time to waste.

"November twenty second, 1963, Dallas, Texas, downtown." I said. Drury was working. He gave me a strange look and said, "Ready?"

Dallas, Texas, November 1963 slowly crept into the room. I was on the curb, in the crowd, just down from the corner and across from the Texas School Depository. I could see a man and a rifle popping in and out of an upper floor window. If I could warn anyone, would I? What Earth would I return to if President Kennedy hadn't been assassinated? It was a moot point. I looked across and down the street and there it was, the grassy knoll. I could solve one mystery, at least. I walked over and surveyed the area. No one was there. The cheering and mayhem ratcheted way up. The motorcade was turning the corner. How close it all seemed. There he was. There she was. They both looked so young and healthy. I started to feel sick and thought I might throw up. I looked up and saw the rifle. Everything was too close.

The assassin could have hit him with a rock if he'd wanted to. I could almost have reached out and touched the car. I'd seen the Zapruder film too many times. I turned to the trees and heard the sickening sound of a rifle blast. Then another and another and another. Loud! The car's engine screamed as it roared past me. Mrs. Kennedy was climbing over the trunk looking confused. Her dress was covered in blood and matter. The car hit a bump and the president's head briefly bobbed up. There was no doubt he was gone immediately. I heard the trees rustle behind me. There was no one there. It was pandemonium on the Dallas street. People were pointing toward the Depository window. I'd seen enough. I knew how this story ended. I stepped out of the scene and looked at Drury. Fade to black.

I know what I needed. The same thing the country needed in 1964. Ladies and gentlemen, The Beatles! What an opportunity. But which Beatles? Shea Stadium? Hamburg? Ed Sullivan? Hollywood Bowl? No. The Cavern, 1962, any Liverpool afternoon. If I came back and didn't take advantage of this opportunity my buddies would string me up. Drury knew what I wanted. Set me up, Dude. He was smiling. He asked if I would show him our music. I think I'd been asked that a few times. Indeed, I would, Drury. Just check this out. It's all you'll ever need to know.

The smoky scene crept in and I was in the middle of the Cavern in all its sweaty, smokey, promise of sex majesty. I'd heard stories of the condensation on the walls and how The Beatles were lucky to not have gotten electrocuted. The walls were dripping. And then I heard it. "Gonna tell Aunt Mary 'bout Uncle John." It was the unmistakable sound of a young McCartney. The Cavern was only about half full as I turned toward the stage and behold...Pete Best. I had to laugh. I should have specified post Pete Best and into the Ringo era. But this was cool, too. They were sporting the German haircuts but certainly not the clean-cut look of The Ed Sullivan Show. The sound was rough, but energetic. As Long Tall Sally went on, the dance floor, for what it was, filled up. I moved up to the front of the stage then onto the stage. The amps were not even quite as good as my high school band's but again, the energy made up for it. I was standing between Paul and George. This alone was worth the price of admission. Pete was keeping a solid beat and there was a group of girls who were decidedly Pete fans.

The rumor was always that Pete was fired because the Beatles were jealous of his popularity. According to producer George Martin, Ringo was a better drummer and the Beatles had already decided to sack him. Either way, they were rockin' today. I got off the stage and took a spot at the back of the room. The Cavern was tiny, and The Beatles were huge. I heard four songs, songs that I could play in my sleep when I noticed an odd-looking guy to my left. He was wearing, oh my God, it was Sam, in the Cavern! Could this possibly get any stranger.

"What do you think?" I said. He replied as most parents did in 1964, "Loud." He asked if I'd seen enough and of course I hadn't but I didn't want to be an ungrateful guest, so I gave him the "Let's go" look. Man, that was a tough room to leave. The Cavern faded away to the strains of "Mr. Postman." All the air seemed to go out of the room. So, the Beatles in the Cavern were really here, in real time? I was assured they were, and also there in real time. Yer' killin' me, Einstein. I thanked Drury for a wonderful afternoon. He asked when I was going to show him music.

I said," You just saw it."

10

Sam was perplexed by the Beatles thing but not too perplexed to eat. We stopped at a small cafe type place at the bottom of the terminal and sat outside on a beautiful stretch of green grass. It was like a large kiosk with tables outside. I heard nature sounds but didn't know what they were or where they were coming from. I was hearing different languages or at least different dialects as we enjoyed a slice of pizza and a flavored water of some kind. There was a good crowd milling around and Sam seemed to be popular.

A lot of interesting looking folks were hanging out, so I wasn't attracting too much attention. It was a beautiful day as all days were. The weather was controlled. Grass, trees, flowers etc. were controlled from underground. Too many questions to even ponder at this point. I could have done the time traveling thing all day; MLK and the Selma bridge, Dinosaurs, Shakespeare, Lincoln's Gettysburg Address, my high school girlfriend cheating on me, the big bang and more, much more Beatles. A woman came over to join us and Sam introduced her as his mate. That was my impression, wife, mate, partner, special friend. I took her hand and held it for a second in an Earth handshake. She had a soft friendly smile and I liked her immediately. She, like Sam, put out a good vibe. "Let's go for a ride," She said.

We walked a short distance to an area where twenty or thirty eggs were. They were sitting about two feet off the ground but in a very solid position. We commandeered one. I asked if this was theirs and got a "No" in unison. They looked at each other and smiled. Aw, ain't that nice. I guess this was like the NYC Citi bikes, pick one up over here and drop it off over there. Sam introduced his wife, but I didn't quite catch or understand her name. She was beautiful with large black eyes. She had a sad, mournful look to her but there was nothing sad or mournful about her. Her hair was very straight and longer than most. She and Sam were working like a well-oiled machine. They were perfect. Preflight checkup completed, Sam looked at me and was that a joking grimace? Bang! We were off! Tearing up and out at a precarious screaming angle. Mrs. Sam was smiling. Sam was hanging on. I was trying to act nonplussed. I was getting pretty good at nonplussed.

It seemed like we were on a joy ride, a high altitude, high speed joy ride. We were at the edge of space and this was my second look at Aldair and its huge continents. Now diving toward its ocean and into its ocean. Well, this is something new, clear water getting darker and darker as we descend. And now going in and around an underwater mountain range. Then interrupting a school of large octopus type creatures that started chasing us. Up and away and back into daylight. A shoreline and a small group of terminals came into view. A right turn and a quick descent to a cool little beach house. I'm home. It looked like one of those woodsy Thomas Kincaid paintings or tapestries, the kind of home inhabited by elves.

The egg skidded to a stop alongside the quaint home. We disembarked and Mr. and Mrs. Sam headed inside. I was pulled to the edge of the beach, alongside Mother Ocean. I smelled salt, so familiar. Aldair was looking more and more like our sister planet. This would be Earth in five hundred years. Hell, I'll bet we can be here in three hundred years. Ms. was looking at me through a large picture window. Sam was walking over. He was saying this was their getaway. They spent a lot of time at their work and needed down time. I would have thought that overpopulation would be a problem. But given the size of Aldair, about one and a half times the size of earth and their moving out to populate planets and moons in their system, they seemed to have made it work. This is our future and our far-reaching future. Planets are born and planets die. Stars are born and stars die. We'll have to eventually become nomads if we can make it that far. The Aldairans have started the process.

I knew that Sam was an" explorer" and proudly wore that hat. I asked Sam what his wife's field was, and he said medical. She was a doctor. We went inside. Kate was cooking, I decided to call her Kate for no apparent reason. She looked like a Kate. No, she looked and sounded like Kate from The Real McCoy's. That was it. What is it with that weird everyone reminds me of someone thing I have, and have always had?

There was a stove top on the wall. It came down and morphed into a continuous stove top on a flat surface. I'd like to see how vertical cooking is done. Sounds risky. There was a refrigerator in the wall. Just beyond the kitchen was a larger room divided by furniture of some kind, like you would use a bookcase to divide spaces. They were just blocks that I was sure served some purpose. There was a small back area where I could see a bed and a smaller room that I hoped was a bathroom. It was.

What's next, I thought? Sam told me I'd be going home tomorrow. I felt odd about that. This was just so interesting, different and unique. How long had it been? I was guessing four earth days. The length of day here would be longer. Or maybe not, depending on the speed of rotation. Look at me getting all scientific. And what was Aldair's relation to its sun? Kate said the Aldairan day was thirty-six hours and their year was only slightly longer than ours. My age calculations were off. They were healthier and had a longer life span than us, so I'd just tack on twenty years to everyone. It was all very confusing. I optimistically asked how our introduction was going to evolve. Would it be a news conference, crashing the White house or a slow cruise around Earth letting everyone get a good look at us? I'd had a nagging feeling for a while. Sam and Kate looked at each other. And not in a good way.

"We'll send you back with your iPad, Sam said. Write this all down. When you're done the pad will return to us. (He called it an iPad. Ha!) Then you'll be on your own. This memory and anything connected to it will fade." Well, that was a swift kick in the stones.

I said, "I thought you'd said, and I quote, it's time we met." Sam said, "And we did. And as time goes on, we'll meet more and more of you. But there will be no grand revelation. This is the way it's being done." I asked if I'd done something wrong. Kate said, "No. You were a perfect ambassador. But this is the way it's done, for now." She looked at Sam. Perfect or not I kind of felt like I was being hung out to dry. But with keeping up the good attitude I simply said. Ok. What's to eat." But this was something else I had to think about.

Kate and I sat outside, and Sam brought out a platter with three large salads and a bottle of something with three glasses. He sat and poured us each a glass. He raised his glass and looked at me. "Toast?" he said. I was getting so used to hearing words and thoughts and words and thoughts turned into impressions that I could understand that I didn't notice how I was receiving information anymore. The drinks were a strong wine that gave me a very unique buzz. Everything seemed clearer, brighter. It was almost hallucinogenic but in an easy familiar way. I decided it was time for the big question. The wine was loosening me up. I just blurted out, "What about life, or lack of it, after death?" Kate, being in the medical field answered, "Would you like to find out? And, of course, we'll bring you back." That was a jaw dropper. How could I pass that up, the almighty ancient question? I gave an enthusiastic, wine stoked nod. Kate said it's nap time and she and Sam disappeared. I went back outside and collapsed in one of the form fitting, all knowing loungers and passed out listening to and smelling the shore break. I could have been down the Jersey Shore.

11

I opened my eyes to a beautiful sunset. The water was very calm, just rippling up to shore. A small catlike, raccoon like, fox like critter was smelling my foot. The shoe part of the wetsuit was removable and anytime I can set my toes free, particularly in sand, or what passes for sand, I'm all in. Was he curious or tasting? I slowly rose and he ran about five feet away, turned for a second and ran into the surf. Interesting. A fish cat type critter combination? I was running out of words. I got up and walked inside. Kate was painting. I asked if I could see. She turned it around. It was me being tasted by the cat fish. The girl was good. She said the cat fish was like the occasional pet but was very shy. They'd leave food out from time to time. Sometimes it'd eat and sometimes it wouldn't. She put down her brushes and gave me the follow me signal. We went back out and around to the side of the house to a small carport type area There was a table and a console. Consoles equaled adventure I was discovering.

"Are you ready for your trip to the other side?" she said in a mock horror movie tone. Where would she get that from? She told me that every civilization at some point discovers the back and forth of life here and life there. It's just a continuation of this but in a different form.

"And all happening now," I said. She laughed and pointed to the table. I lay down.

Kate said, "Once the way is discovered it tends to get overused, at first, which is not the design. We're supposed to make the most of here and they're supposed to make the most of there. So, after the initial interest only the occasional visitor, like you, will drop in. We stand out over there. They humor us but have no interest in a lot of contact. And rarely will one of them come here." I wasn't sure if I wanted to know the answer but asked, once there, what's the plan?

Kate said there are any number of paths, but she didn't want to go too deep. This whole trip was a conglomeration of small, wonderful open-ended visions. Here comes another one. Kate looked down at me. "Ready?" I had to laugh. "No," I thought, but said nothing.

"By the way, she said, this will be your afterlife, the earth afterlife, not ours."

Before I could digest that I was floating above my body and being pulled toward a misty carnival looking area. I had read so many life after life experiences that I thought I'd be ready for whatever might occur. I wasn't. It was suddenly all too clear. Everything. I thought I heard the odd but welcoming sound of a calliope. As my eyes adjusted, I saw that it was one large, brilliant light and the sound was the sound of me moving. I reached and became the light. It was me; I was it and we were everything I'd ever known. The sense of movement stopped. The light was still there but became a part of everything. I was standing in a field. There was a bridge in front of me. I felt wonderful. There were groups of people, earth people, on the other side of the bridge and a city far beyond. The city was sparkling. I guess I was dead. I didn't feel dead, whatever that's supposed to feel like. I looked at my arms and hands. They were the arms and hands of a young man. I was wearing a white robe. I looked behind me and saw the residue that was left by the light. It seemed alive, as if it had delivered me and was moving on while at the same time leaving an imprint. It felt like an old friend. It was an old friend. This doesn't make sense but at the time it made immaculately perfect sense.

I realized the city looked like the city beyond the terminals on Aldair. But it wasn't a city at all. It was glittering mountains that also seemed alive. Everything seemed alive; the grass I was standing on, the river running under the bridge and even the sky. Everything seemed to be breathing and celebrating. I also had a real sense of home. I wanted to get to the other side of the bridge and headed that way.

An older gentleman was crossing the bridge and coming toward me. I say older because compared to everyone else, myself included, he was. He looked to be about fifty with slicked back grayish hair and a red face. I knew him but from where I could not remember. I'd stopped walking and he met me on my side of the bridge.

He spread his arms wide and said, "Hey Teddy! Curious, are we?" He looked at me for a minute and seemed to understand everything.

He said "You can't stay here, you know." I felt sad, but not an earthly sad. I knew my sadness was somehow a step to ultimate happiness. I'm not exactly sure what that means but I did at the time. I wanted to stay. I was home. People on the other side of the bridge were looking at me. They knew me and I knew them, really knew them. My greeter looked at me. Who was he and why did he call me Teddy, a Plainfield connection?

"Well, you almost made it here twice before but 'twas not to be." My grandmother would use words like 'twas and 'twill. A Newfoundland thing? As I was pondering the "almost made it here before" comment, a TV set, with rabbit ears, appeared on a table in front of me. Rabbit ears? Heaven has bad reception? On what looked like an old black and white television appeared, in glorious color, me.

I was surfing alone in the evening on Long Beach Island, NJ. I knew what was about to happen. I caught a wave, my board immediately nosedived, flipped out of the water and headed to shore without me. This was a time before anyone used leashes. I was tired and caught in a riptide. I had a thought that this could be it for your hero and for a second, gave in. The shore looked so far away. Then I had a feeling that it was my choice to live or die. I chose live. I swam underwater toward the shore and when I came up, completely shot but within swimming distance of shore and out of the rip, there was my Morey Pope surfboard right next to me. The nose had snapped off, but we made it in together. I'd had a few close calls while surfing or body surfing. Watching folks on the shore running, laughing and tossing a frisbee while you're in a death match is frightening, frustrating and slightly grounding. Keeping your cool is everything. Finally walking out of the water is glorious.

In the movie "The End," Burt Reynolds is on a mission to kill himself. In a final attempt he walks into Mother Ocean and swims out to where he's sure he can't make it back. He does a deep dive and comes up screaming, "I want to live!!"On the way back in he makes deals with God. Among them, "If you let me live, Lord, I'll give ya fifty percent of everything I make!" As he gets closer, "I'll follow the Ten Commandments. Thou shalt not commit adultery. Thou shalt not…. Thou shalt not…. I'll learn the Ten Commandments, God" And closer, "I'll give ya twenty five percent of everything I make. I'm talkin' gross, Lord!" He makes it and the brink of death promises are still there but take a back seat. I've done that. We've probably all done that.

The picture on the TV rippled and zapped and there I was in my apartment in Pittstown, NJ. I'd been replacing the glass in a broken window while standing on a hornet's nest. Don't try it. I beat the bees inside and did the old Boy Scout remedy of applying mud to my foot. It wasn't working. Breathing was difficult. I caught a glimpse of myself in the bathroom mirror and I was a sheet. I lay down on the bed feeling very peaceful. The window was broken, I'd knocked my pedal steel guitar over and my hand, from the broken glass, had bled all over me and the rug. It was a scene, man. I thought in a couple of hours, tomorrow or the next day, someone is going to walk in on this and wonder what the hell happened. My breathing was getting slower and slower. I just waited. It slowly picked up and I came around. I had a whopping headache and some cleaning up to do but I was back. The doc said because I'd gotten it in the foot and not higher up, I was able to wait it out. I've since gotten an epi pen that I rarely carry. The TV fizzled and faded. Technically I wasn't dead so why the life review? I didn't feel sad anymore. I felt enlightened, uplifted and incredibly lucky.

I looked at my companion. "Spread the good news," he said. Jubilantly. Whoa! It was Uncle Jack! Uncle Jack was one of my grandfather's brothers. I mentioned him earlier. He came from Newfoundland and every few years he and/or his other brother Len would drop into my grandparent's home on Monroe Ave in Plainfield, right next door to us. Uncle Jack was missing an arm. How that happened I've either forgotten or never knew. Some years later I saw a film that my grandmother had of Uncle Jack seeming to be giving a speech. He was standing on a rock at the end of a jetty, obviously Newfoundland. There was no sound, but he was animatedly making a point about something. His stump of an arm gave an odd appearance to the scene. Even my grandmother was chuckling, then, as my grandfather came into the picture, crying, then chuckling. I liked Uncle Jack. He was a friendly sort of chap. I have a journal that my grandfather had done on a visit back home. It was extremely detailed, and that trip must have been the source of the film.

Uncle Len was a likable rogue. I think my grandmother had some reservations about him but that all went over my head. Uncle Len's main concern seemed to be finding someone to accompany him to the Clinton Tavern. Then he'd find me, take me over to gram's and intone, "It's ony me". (That's the correct spelling. Uncle Len was channeling me, and I was no linguist at five.) Who could refuse entry to this lovable pair? My grandmother couldn't.

As my recognition of Uncle Jack became clear, a miraculous thing happened. It was as if the top of my head was lifted and all the mysteries of the universe were being poured in. Second by second, I was learning, becoming aware. Space, time, science, music, mathematics, past, present and all the trails and repercussions of my life connections were becoming more and more clear. It was wonderful and overwhelming. I saw that everything was, is, and will be fine. No regrets. No fear. I received an answer to everything including my all-encompassing question of "why all the suffering," man's inhumanity to man, the illnesses of children, debilitating diseases, the wretched existence of so many animals, endless wars and on and on. All questions were answered in a second in a matter of fact manner. It was obvious. It had to be that way.

Before I could say anything or enjoy and reflect on my newfound knowledge, Uncle Jack ceremoniously raised his hand, of which there were two, and with a smile and a wink, sent me off. Thanks for the warning. Just before I was whisked away from my heavenly realm I glanced over to my right and there were dogs I'd known and loved. There was no Rainbow Bridge but the whole group, maybe seven or eight, were on a large gazebo floating in the middle of a glorious, sparkling pond. There were two cats sitting on the railing looking rather disinterested. I knew them, too. They were acting too cool for the room, but I could feel the love. A walkway connected the gazebo to the other shore. There was one dog sitting there looking at me very compassionately, a dog I hadn't been very kind to. He was full of forgiveness and I wanted to run over and hug him. I'd be seeing them all again. That alone was worth the trip.

Then it was as if a string attached to the middle of my back was sprung and I hurtled backward through what I can only call the universe, then a blue sky and then a thud. Kate said I lay there for a minute or two. I came around feeling joyous. I hoped I could hang onto this feeling. I have, except for that secrets of the universe thing. That's gone. But with a little bit of conjuring I can get a piece of it back every now and then. Thanks Uncle Jack. I could absolutely see the temptation to do that all the time. I also recognized why it couldn't or shouldn't be done all the time and why I was given the view of my "close encounters." Life has a fragility that needs to be appreciated and not taken for granted. The order of the universe.

12

We went inside. It was getting dark now. Kate and Sam weren't being very talkative. I felt they were being deferential to me and the experience I'd just had. It was akin to the back in the day post "trip," the time to reflect or absorb and try to recognize what, if anything, you got out of it. There was no need to talk about or dissect it unless you wanted to. I felt a lightness and a heaviness. I was very alert and wasted at the same time. I looked out the large picture window and thought, "What a beautiful night." Sam said something very softly and the walls and ceiling disappeared. They were still there but they weren't. The stars were brilliant, and I could see the foam of the surf break. Three of the cat/foxes were about ten feet away just sitting. Kate walked near them and tossed nuggets of food. Soft music was playing, like nothing I'd ever heard. I didn't have to show them anything. They had music. It was beautiful and seemed to be coming from the universe. Something sounded odd. The music had no time. There was no 1-2-3-4. It made me feel like I was still "over there."

Kate said, "A part of you still is, and always will be. Keep it with you." I never wanted to leave this moment. Then I was alone. Where'd everyone go?

I heard, "We're here. Contemplate." I think that's what I heard. And so, I did.

The Jerry Garcia/Robert Hunter tune Uncle John's Band starts, "The first days are the hardest days, don't you worry anymore. 'Cause when life looks like easy street there is danger at your door. Think this through with me. Let me know your mind. Wo- oh what I want to know - o is are you kind." Kindness. It's everything. I like to believe I have a kindness about me. I hope I do. I've been told I do. That's the ultimate compliment. I remember taking heat from my jock friends for hanging out with the Chess Club guys.

I didn't care. I got heat from my hippie friends for hanging out with the jocks. I didn't care. I got heat from everyone for dating a girl who, I guess, was not the most attractive woman but was possibly the sweetest person I'd ever met. And I think I let her get away because of peer pressure. I should have had one of those machines that has the rope you pull, and a foot comes up and boots you in the ass. I could've used that on more than one occasion. I've come to recognize the real importance of kindness in my later life. Better late than never? Looks, wit, wealth are all nice. But it's all about the kindness, the humanity. My latest adventure drove the point home. Reflect on that. I haven't been that kind. There are animals I wasn't kind to. There are people I wasn't kind to. Maybe no more than anyone else but I wish I could go back and do some things over. As Vito Corleone says, "This is the life we have chosen." Indeed. Except for the guy in the video back on the ship who seemed to have somewhat of an attitude, I've encountered nothing but kindness. I hope this is our future.

Something was walking toward me. It was Sam and he was carrying a large stone, almost as large as him. He carefully placed it just outside the perimeter of this deck, patio, sitting area. I got up and walked over. He had a satisfied look on his face. The stone was sculpted into something I didn't recognize but it was four feet of coolness. How'd he carry that? He grinned at me and peeled off his arms! They were actually sleeves that covered his arms and allowed him to do things like that. He left for a moment and came back with what resembled thin sweatpants. He told me to put these on and run. I did, and ran, like the wind. Man, that felt good. I was sixteen again and running across Rivercrest Park and I wasn't getting tired. How? I didn't know how far I ran and hoped I could find my way back. As I was running the fox/raccoon critters were running alongside me. I poured it on and left them in the dust.

I flashed back to a day at Rivercrest Park. It was one of our hundreds of neighborhood football games and I was having one of those days. I punted a ball that went as high and far as any I'd ever kicked. It must have gotten caught in the wind. I couldn't drop a pass. I outran my pal Rock. I could never outrun Rock. I caught a pass and he was chasing me. We were neck and neck and finally he said, "F**k it!" I beat Rock! I'll never forget that day. I was sixteen and I look back and think that may have been my physical peak. Till now. I must have run full tilt for three miles and wasn't winded. I gotta get a pair of these. Running's a beautiful thing. I didn't miss it till I couldn't do it.

Check out the Burt Lancaster movie "Jim Thorpe – All American." Burt portrays native American athlete

Jim Thorpe, Olympian, football player and baseball player who got screwed out of his Olympic medals because he received money to play baseball one summer. They were posthumously returned but it left a bitter residue. The opening scene is a young Jim running home, across fields, jumping streams and fences. He arrives home winded and exhilarated reveling in his youthful physicality. It's a beautiful scene. When I was around forty, I went out to dinner with my Aunt Catherine, Katrine (remember her?) her second husband, the ever curmudgeonly, Mike, my brother and sister and my soon to be wife, Donna. During dinner somehow the topic of age and ability came up and Mike announced that he didn't think I could run anymore. I respectfully disagreed. After dinner we were all standing outside, and I said I'd go get the car and took off running. I pulled a hamstring. I tried not to show it but I had to slow to a limpy jog. I later confessed to my sister that Mike was right. I couldn't run anymore. I wish Mike could have seen see me chugging down the Aldairan beach tonight!

I recognized Sam's chachki and pulled up to their home with the critters on my tail. No one was around. I pulled off the jet pants, used the facilities, ordered a slice of pizza and a water and collapsed on a couch that, of course, molded to my body in a most comfortable manner. The suit kept me going but my body recognized it was shot. I wanted to go home. Kate appeared from somewhere and said, "You'll start you trip back to Earth tomorrow. Sleep." She was transparent. Hologram? I was too tired to think and passed out.

Part 7

**

1

I woke up well rested and sore. I was tired last night. A "good" tired as we used to say. The walls and ceiling were back, and a magnificent sunrise was shining through the large beachfront window. I had that last day of vacation feeling. I was thinking that I may have really blown it. I should have spent more time asking questions, just sat Sam or anyone down and interrogated them. Things were happening too quickly. Like a cat with a string my earthy brain was constantly being distracted, pulled in different directions. The Aldairans were willing to answer any inquiries, if somewhat cryptically, but they didn't offer a whole lot. Their primary interest seemed to be allowing me to see and feel, to experience the knowledge that our brothers and sisters will be there when we need them. We're not alone. It's ok. I watched a good chunk of their history and it was very similar to ours. and why wouldn't it be? After the initial WOW, the last couple of days had been the most interesting and enlightening. But it also all felt normal, the way it should be, will be. The first spacewalk was thrilling but there was no Close Encounters, Space Odyssey mind melting, heavenly choir Kumbaya moment. Maybe that was due to the lack of a soundtrack. I remember thinking something about that during the walk, but it was getting hard to remember. The music in movie scenes is what pulls you in, makes you weep, jump, or take the person's hand next to you. The lack of soundtrack gives everything a stunning realness. The ant person, the large, disconnected space head and any species that comes into being starts at point A and has to find a sustaining path through B, C and D. Maybe within the vastness of the universe there are any number of the hundreds of thousands of possible intelligences for whom there's a different path. I can't imagine what that would be, but I was only seeing the elephant's tail. The Aldairans were simply living their lives. I was ready to continue living mine.

I'm not a religious guy but as the lazily religious say, "I'm spiritual." I start every day off with," Thank you for this day, Lord. Thank you." That's it. It makes me feel good. I'm a lucky guy. I don't have or want a lot, but I have everything I need, and then some. I think we all do, have everything we need, that is. Recognize it. I'll quote, again, two of the poets of our time, Mick and Keith. "You can't always get what you want, but if you try some time, you'll find, you get what you need." Thirty or so years ago I was looking down the road wishing/hoping/planning for life to take certain directions. What they were I'll keep to myself, but I realized one day that I had everything I'd hoped for. And anything I didn't have was my own fault. The words for the thanks I'll have to give for this incredible opportunity have not yet been created.

I'd neglected my journal, but I hoped the trip back would afford me the time for that. I had the feeling I'd be on my own once I got back. I had to find out more about that. Would I even remember? There are two kinds of people, the kind that hold their cell phones up during concerts and the kind that watch the concert. I'm the latter. I would rather have the memory than the video. But that's just me. Maybe I'd get no answers, have no white house lawn landing and have nothing except what's in my head for apparently as long as that lasts. Either way will be ok. At least I'll have Linda as a witness. How did she explain this away? There was a small lizard on the wall looking at me with the goofiest look on his face, very quizzical. Like "What the hell are you?" Hey, except for the stubby arms and body topped off with this bulbous head I think I'm a lot like everyone else around here. He disappeared. Great. One more question I'll forget to ask.

2

Sam and Dave were at the egg's controls, the static iPad hanging solidly in space. I was tucked behind the barrier furiously writing anything and everything. My last morning on Aldair had been uneventful. Kate, Sam and I had breakfast on the beach. I had wonderful pancakes, tasteless sausage and run of the mill toast. Good coffee, though. They really had the hang of coffee. They didn't drink it, but their food producer knew how to make it. They'd been making the effort to get the earth food thing right and they were well on their way. It didn't appear, regardless of Rod Serling's predictions, that we were to be on the menu, at least not the Aldairan menu.

Artificial Intelligence was firmly planted in their present and seems to be our future. Again, we are adaptable creatures. Sam had implied that Aldair and Earth would be having more and more interaction in the upcoming years. I didn't like the word years. How about days or weeks?

Sam and Kate had breakfast drinks of some kind. I just realized I hadn't seen any Aldairans eating, just drinking. Did I miss it? Did they not eat? Did I see it? Things were becoming vague. They must eat. Well I got an answer. I had the question and asked. One down. Kate filled me in. They do eat but prefer to get their nutrition from drinks. Along with their emotions their taste buds had gone away. Both were returning. They seemed to enjoy watching me eat and always asked if I enjoyed it, if it tasted like home. At first, I was giving the polite answer but thought I'd better give it to them straight if my Earth mates would be following. Pizza, coffee and cereal, good. Pancakes and chicken salad, bad. Over breakfast I broke the news to Sam and he made a notation on a pad that seemed to literally appear out of thin air. They wanted to get it right. I'd changed into another wetsuit that had a different insignia on the front. I had no idea or interest, really, in what it meant. Had I been promoted? Demoted? I'm not a fashion guy but I think even I'd get tired of the same old look after a while. They didn't seem to. Maybe once they're emotions were fully restored; they'd get some fashion sense.

I gave Kate a thank you and a hug which seemed to put her off. As we were preparing to hop into Sam's ride she came up and gave me a big hug and smile and said clearly, "Now that you know where the place is drop in anytime." Where'd she get that? Aldairan Google? She put out a cool vibe. I liked her. Sam looked perplexed. We got in and shot off.

We were traveling in Sam's two-person egg and I assumed at some point we would be switching to a more substantial ride. My assumption was confirmed about fifteen minutes later as we arrived at another Mother Ship. This one was a brilliant green color with flashing lights all around. It was smaller than Mother one and two but still very substantial. Aldair had slipped out of view after about five minutes. Except for the few large land masses, it really was a brother/sister Earth. We'll meet again. We pulled into the docking area, got out and Sam led me to a comfortable little room and asked if I'd mind waiting there. I didn't mind. He returned about twenty minutes later with Dave in tow. I'd been writing on the iPad, shrunk it and got up to greet Dave. He gave me the hippie handshake and we were off.

3

I'd lost track of time. Everybody seemed to be doing their own thing. I was having a hard time catching my breath. I went over to mention this to Dave. He tweaked the little chest control and once again that sweet Higgins Home for Funerals aroma was permeating my olfactory. I was standing by the floor to ceiling window and noticed we were in the blackness of the void. We'd left the Aldairan system and were now in the massive void before Alpha Centauri. I think this is where we had first encountered the Mother Ship on the way out. I wasn't sure. If so, this was also where we encountered the large floating head of unknown origin.

I just came out and asked if I could have a last spacewalk. They looked at each other and gave me the go ahead. Sam pointed toward the helmet which I didn't realize in the newfangled suit I was wearing was neatly tucked in back below my neck, like a retractable hood. I reached back and it easily came up and over my head morphing into a solid form fitting helmet. Well, this was new. Gloves were applied and I was ready. I thanked the guys for this opportunity. I meant everything. The whole enchilada. I realized we'd be saying goodbye shortly and I was gripped by an overwhelming sadness. I was trying to tell them how much meeting them has meant to me and tried to convey my appreciation to and for them. I didn't know what the future held but assumed I'd never see them again. As mentioned, I'm a Pisces, emotional, watery and full of these feelings. I've said a number of times on my radio show after a particularly cerebral song has finished," I think I'm half chick. Some estrogen apparently got mixed in with my testosterone." I usually get a call or email from a woman reminding me that "chick" is not a cool word. I'm afraid I ignore it. I wanted to give Sam and Dave the bro hug forgetting that their emotions were just slowly returning, and they'd have no idea what I was doing.

I said," Thank you and I'm incredibly grateful that we met." Man, that just didn't say it. Sam came over and held me by the shoulders looking into my eyes. Then Dave came over and held me by the shoulders looking into my eyes. Was this the equivalent of an Aldairan bro hug? I felt a little embarrassed and said," What's the weather like out there?"

Dave said, with a straight face," It's a vacuum." Oh well.

They gave me the once over, said I'd be on my own for a while and led me to the exit which I assumed was in front of me. Trust. I asked how long. This always took a second as they translated time into parameters I could understand.

Sam said," About twenty minutes. Ready?" Before I could acknowledge I was gently sucked out into the blackest black of the void. There were no stars here. Just black. I didn't see them leave but I knew they were gone.

4

I wondered how much of a pain in the ass I was to Sam and Dave. Was I like the irritable little brother with whom they were forced to hang out or was there at least a curiosity or maybe an affection like that for a cute, or not so cute pet? I was thinking they may do this on a regular basis, say hello, get to know, and say goodbye. During my tenure in Bermuda with The Firecreek Band I got pretty friendly with a few guys and asked each of them at different times how they felt about getting to know people; tourists, bands etc. and then after a week or month saying goodbye, knowing they'd probably never see them again. The answer I got from everyone I asked was the same. "You get used to it." I've been back to Bermuda three times since our gig in the eighties and always looked up my pals. I hope to get there one more time before the final curtain.

This spacewalk had a darker feeling than the previous one. When I'd get into an "Are they out there" discussion and the question "Then why haven't we met them?" would come up, one of my theories would be that maybe they can't reach us. And maybe that was part of the master plan. Distance was the barrier. The Aldairans seemed to jump that barrier but maybe inter galactic travel would be the no go. Tool around your own galaxy but no further. The Aldairans had a full ship on their way out of the Milky Way, two ships if I remember correctly. What would they find? And would they ever be able to let anyone know?

5

Something felt odd, different. I felt like I was being watched. I heard a ripping sound. How? No sound in space, right? "No one can hear you scream in space." A chill went right up my back. Something was behind me. By throwing my arms I was able to turn around. It/he was back. The giant apparition of the head. But rather than being here he was on the other side of a divide. Space had been ripped. The "fabric" of space had been ripped! He distorted from the giant piggy/human cartoon head into a human, sporting jeans and a t shirt. He was standing in a large room with a white ceiling and hideous wallpaper. There was a vintage dining room table next to him at which he elegantly sat down. He waved me in and in I went. I floated over to a chair and as gravity returned, I landed with a soft thud. He said, "Take your hat off. Stay awhile!" What the hell was going on? I trusted Sam and Dave. This situation I was not so sure. I sat there. He pointed to my helmet. I pulled it back and was breathing air, or a close facsimile thereof. He looked like a cross between Mitch Miller and Jerry Garcia. He was slim with a white goatee and longish white hair. The white t shirt had a dark blue peace sign in the middle. The jeans were faded and darned if he wasn't wearing Frye boots. I liked him but who and where was he?

"Hungry?" he asked. Well, hell, I've been all in so far. My throat was very dry but I croaked," I could eat." A butler walked in with a tray of food. Well, of course. He put down a platter with tacos and burritos and a bowl of Mexican rice. There was a cooler on the floor next to me. I knew what was in it. I reached in and pulled out two icy beers. They were Coronas, already opened. I passed one to my host. We clicked bottles and I took a swallow. I grabbed a burrito and thought I'd wait for him to take the lead. This had to be some kind of weird dream.

"I'm Lucas, he said. Thanks for joining me." We could have been sitting in a southern California hacienda. I was hungry.

I said, "Thanks for inviting me," and took a large bite of one of the tastiest burritos I'd ever laid lip to. I took another bite and a large swig of the Corona.

I said, "So...." and let it hang there in, wherever we were. Lucas gave a small choking sound as his mouth was full of taco, slapped the table and started laughing and snorting enthusiastically. I thought I had questions before. He waved about the room and asked, "How'd I do?"

"Almost perfect, I said. We need guacamole and chips." Jeeves returned a few seconds later with, of course, guacamole and chips, well above average guacamole and chips. I took another bite of burrito and placed a few chips on my plate. The plate had a grand blue design going all the way around the edge. Where had I seen that before? I took a gulp of Corona, grabbed a few chips and sat back. Lucas took a swig, also sat back with a large grin, and began.

"You, he said, are an interesting group. Much more so than the Aldairans. Nice people but not a lotta heart, the Aldairans, I mean. You can be a vicious lot but also extremely loving and caring. That has to make for a chaotic existence. Some survive that. Some don't. I'm thinking you're gonna make it. And I like your fashion, and food. Pass over some chips, please." I almost felt like I was going to pass out, again. This was above and beyond.

"What else!" he said. I just ran with it.

"Well the fashion may be considered a little outdated. Not for me, you understand. I'm an old hippie. But that's vintage 1960's flower power garb. You wear it well. I'm taking a shot. The look is for my benefit?" A pause, then I was sitting across from what looked to be a bright neon light with a deformed, somewhat human form inside. It was not sitting but floating just above the chair, pulsing at irregular intervals. I heard in a high watery computer type generated voice "Better?"

"That's very cool, I said, but could we go back to vintage?" An audible pop and my host was back. I was really getting good at the unfazed countenance, but this was challenging. I took another belt of Corona and a bite of burrito.

"Where are you from," I asked.

"Here, there and everywhere, he said. You visited The Beatles on your excursion."

I replied, "Very nice, but that doesn't answer my question." He said, "I haven't eaten, or spoken in a long time. I forgot how enjoyable it can be. We can't let the little things get lost in our existence. "Like rolling in the grass, or climbing a tree," Was he quoting me?

"Or hugging a dog?" I said. Did I just see a wink?

Taking a large bite of a taco he said," Or eating! But to answer your question, and I know you've heard a lot of this, but we really are from everywhere and anywhere. Ha! And to make it more confusing...... anytime. It's all linear. We had our "enlightenment" about four and a half million years ago. We've mapped the entire universe, and beyond. We like to mess with people, like the Aldairans, just to let them know that there's a lot more out there, give them something to shoot for. The more negative forces we stay away from. We're giving you a little something extra."

"Where are we? I asked.

"We are currently four hundred and fifty thousand galaxies away from your Milky Way, give or take." he said. For a second, I thought I might throw up. I didn't.

I said, "You obviously know all about us," holding up a chip loaded with guacamole.

"At this point we know all about everything, he said. A minute percentage make it this far, but it makes for a grand community when they do. That's the plan, and the hope."

I asked, So what's your role?"

"To guide, help, educate, enjoy a good taco and a cold beer," he said. He stood up and motioned me to follow him. We walked through a door and into a magnificent night, stars too many to take in immediately. There was a large moon, four or five times closer than ours and two smaller moons. There were a group of large clear globes floating in the sky. I couldn't tell how far away they were. They could have been fifty miles away or a thousand miles away. They were filled with sparkles.

Lucas said," Cities."

"What?" I said.

"Not exactly, but you understand the concept, right? He said. The sparkles you see are cities, of a kind, and they're far, far away. The globes are the evolution of planets. I've simplified it. You're just not smart enough to get it." He laughed as he put his hand on my shoulder. I felt a strong transfer of energy.

"Well, thanks, man," I said.

He continued, "Not your fault. And it's all relative. In your, and ours and everyone's development there was the guy who discovered that striking two rocks together created a spark which formed fire. Wink. That increased the diet options, leading to a stronger, healthier species and, bam, we're eating tacos and burritos in a galaxy far, far away. And thanks for the guacamole and chips tip. They're delicious. So compared to us, or the Aldairans, or you, the rock banger was not that bright. But that day he was. That day he was enlightened. He felt a spark, recognized a spark and took the next step of bringing that spark to life. And the doors started to open. See?"

I looked around. We were in an area that resembled the Southwest of the United States. I once spent a night on a blind date that worked out well on a mountaintop in the desert a few miles outside El Paso, Texas. The deserts of the Southwest are mystical, spiritual. Along with the brilliance of the nighttime sky, the sounds of unseen wildlife, out there, and close by, demand a respect that if not given, can be unforgiving. The southwest Texas nights were stunning. They rivaled, or possibly surpassed, this. Minus the hanging cities.

Lucas seemed to be enjoying the evening, taking it all in. There was a large range of mountains in the distance and foothills closer by. I stepped back and got a better look at the dwelling. It looked like one of those small log homes that are built from kits and there was smoke coming from a chimney. I hadn't noticed a fireplace. There was nothing, absolutely nothing else around. I asked Lucas if he lived here and he said, Sometimes, when I get the urge or if it's convenient. Like now."

"It's beautiful, I said. Looks like home."

He said, "It's all home." All the mysterious references were challenging my feeble brain, which was feeling feebler the longer I stayed. After all, I was only a C student.

I walked around to the other side and, of course, there was a hot tub. Lucas was already naked and jumped in, beer in hand. I have no issue with any lifestyle but it felt a tad odd. Oh well, when in Rome. I got naked and hopped in, beer in hand. Lucas had his head back, enjoying the stars. I did the same, from the other side of the tub. This was all too real to be a dream. It had none of the properties of a dream. It was just too clear. Do I keep saying that?

"You're a musician, he said. "In the early part of your century I played with a jazz band on and off for about a year in Kansas City." I just let that hang there, not sure if he was ribbing me or not. He didn't seem to be.

"Keep it up, he said. "It's good for the soul."

What instrument did you play?" I said waiting for a quick response.

"Cornet." he quickly answered. That made sense. The old school name for trumpet. We both settled back. Eight or nine shooting stars made an appearance. Was that for my benefit? I put a small amount of the hot tub water in my mouth and spit it out. It was chlorinated water. Nailed it again.

"When you wish upon a star...." Lucas sang.

"Makes no difference who you are," I answered.

Lucas said," He was ahead of his time, don't you think?" I'd seen "Fantasia" with a few pals while enjoying the merits of Orange Sunshine.

I said, "No, he was right of his time. We were of the wrong time." I wasn't sure what that meant but I could be as cryptic as the next guy.

"Now you're getting it," he said. I lay back in the welcoming warmth of the interstellar hot tub while Lucas filled my head with many, but not all, of the secrets of the universe. It all just made so much freakin' sense! I'd already forgotten the download I received from the other side, except for the brief snippets, and how long they would last was anyone's guess.

Lucas said, "Yeah, sorry. You won't remember this either."

I said, maybe a little too loud," Then why tell me?"

"Interesting conversation, no? Lucas said. "Wouldn't you rather know the secrets of the universe for ten minutes than not at all?"

I took a cold swallow and emphatically said, "Yes." I had no idea how much time had passed but it had to be at least an hour or more. The fellas would be looking for me. I felt that Lucas, if needed, could probably get me back home. He hopped out and ran around to the front of the log home. I climbed out, was immediately dry, popped on the wetsuit and followed.

When I came around the corner Lucas was wearing an iridescent sharkskin suit, had his hair slicked back and was leaning against a lamppost that was not there before. Stopped me in my tracks.

"Very Goodfellas," I said.

He thought for a second and said, "That's what I was goin' for."

I had the feeling this was coming to an end and asked if I could share this with Sam and Dave. Lucas said he preferred that I didn't, that with the relativity of time and all they wouldn't even have missed me. That answered my next question. He was back to the hippie look. The lamppost was gone. He was giving me the peace sign.

"Buckle up," he said. I was sad to leave this guy. He was the heppest of cats and put out the coolest of vibes.

"See you again?" I asked as I snapped my helmet back into place and replaced the attached gloves.

"Probably not," he said. "But maybe I'll tune you in every now and then." I received a strong message of brotherhood, share the love, we are all in this together, and everything will not only be all right, everything is all right. I shot back a thanks for the interesting repast but before I could finish, a clap of thunder and a flash of some kind and I was back in the void watching Lucas from the other side. He was still holding the peace sign up and danged if he wasn't giving me the "raspberry" at the same time. An actual zipper came down and closed up the "fabric of space." What a pisser.

6

I had no idea but hoped that I was close to where Sam and Dave had left me. I saw something float by, bubbles of some kind. It was frozen beer globules and just out of my reach was the Corona beer bottle that had been in my hand on my sudden departure. Great. Interstellar littering. How would I explain that? Maybe they wouldn't notice. Man, I was alone. I mean alone! No stars, moons, planets, no nothin'! This, the space between stars, felt like a place where no one was supposed to be, a no man's land. Was it a cosmic dividing line? Could or should nothing be out here? Was a star needed to give off a welcoming kind of energy conducive to all the constants of life and habitation? Ours certainly did. I was anxious to see it again.

Mother Sun, like Mother Ocean had its own healing qualities. Besides just feeling good, warming and invigorating on a nice spring day, it's loaded with Vitamin D, essential for the human form in any number of ways. Our sun is at a perfect distance and delivers just the right amount of energy to support our beautiful Earth and all its creatures. So, this is all an interconnected puzzle that works beautifully. I'd understood it all precisely while I was with Lucas but the download he'd given me was wearing off, a kind of "Flowers for Algernon" thing. Between my glimpse of the afterlife and "My Dinner with Lucas," I was gaining and losing a helluva lot of knowledge. "Que sera."

7

I was doing front and back somersaults, side rolls and just having a rollickin' good time. I felt alone in the universe. The beer bottle was out of sight. I didn't feel good about that, but it would have to be my secret. I wish I'd had an opportunity to put a note in it.

I felt, before I saw, the egg approaching from directly in front of me. Like in my yard days before, it was a dot then it was here. It was a larger egg and there were two additional beings inside. As the egg pulled up in front of me the newbies were staring. The craft pulled up and eased me in. Contact. Dave asked if I'd had a good time and I was cautiously discreet. Of the new guys one was short and chubby while the other was tall and very thin. I didn't know Aldairans could be chubby but so be it. The long arms looked a little odd on a stubby body. Then again, what were they making of me.

Sam introduced two more Aldairan names I couldn't pronounce so they were henceforth Abbott and Costello. I was running out of what little creativity I had left. Sam said they had never met Benjamin Franklin and were anxious to have an opportunity to really interact with a human. I don't recall ever being ogled before, but I promise I'll never do it to anyone again. They were very friendly and extremely curious.

This egg had a larger seating area and I pulled up a seat and removed my helmet and gloves. I immediately felt sick. Abbott reached over and tweaked the tweaker and all was fine once again. Dave mentioned there was food available if I'd like. I was still full from "lunch" and just thanked him and said maybe later. He gave me an odd head tilt and nodded. I had relieved myself during the "walk" on my return from Lucas' place so I was set, I thought, for the duration.

Abbott and Costello sat on either side of me and after asking if it was ok started peppering me with questions. They wanted to know about love and hate, war and peace, baseball, football, music, dancing, movies, comedy and on and on. They seemed noticeably young, kind of like college kids and had that youthful enthusiasm that embodies, well, youth. Dave was engrossed in something, but Sam was watching bemusedly. He walked over and with a napkin of some kind wiped something off my mustache. It was green. I wiped a little more off and, yup, it was guacamole.

"Well, would ya look at that," I said. Sam brought it over to Dave. Dave stopped what he was doing and touched the wall. A small plate materialized. The napkin was placed on the plate and it retracted. Some hieroglyphs popped up and the fellas couldn't hide their surprise. Meanwhile A and C were still firing away but I was only half listening and answering at this point. They were having a tough time with the concept of competition, in all its forms, sports, academics etc. Especially when it came to kids, they just thought it was so wrong. Why compete? Why not work together for the greater good? I told them check in with us in a decade or two as competition was slowly fading and we'd soon all be the same.

I wasn't a fan of the trophies for all idea but I don't have kids so I could only see it second hand. I did have many conversations during trips to the airport with corporate employers who were not impressed with the crop of workers coming out of college. They were using words like entitled, unmotivated and not prepared for the demands of a competitive job market. The people I saw that were making a mark were basically working or available 24/7. There may be a happy medium. I think the current crop coming out of college, the millennials, may just see a better and possibly more efficient way to do things.

I've met a number of successful corporate types during my chauffeur tenure who were where they were simply because they had to pay for the huge house that they never saw. They might kiss their wife and kids' goodbye on Monday and see them again on Friday while being on call all weekend. And they were miserable. On the other hand, there were men and women who embraced that lifestyle and lived it for all it was worth. They were the ones who were having a hard time with the millennials. The one for all and all for one seemed to work for the Aldairans. Maybe that's where we end up. It doesn't seem like a bad place.

There's been a strong implication that either I won't be getting any help here vis a vis first contact or I may, at the very least, experience severe memory loss regarding the situation. It was all very confusing. But it reminded me to get back to writing, particularly regarding "My Dinner with Lucas." I asked Abbott and Costello if we could take a break and they reluctantly agreed. I popped out the iPad and got to writing. I realized that if and when I had to surrender the iPad, they would read all about the Lucas encounter. So be it. I'd try to be vague. A and C moved away. Sam came over and asked if I'd like some guacamole. I said sure if I could get some chips. The jig was up. He inquired where I'd run into guacamole out here. I was prepared to do a song and dance about how I had brought some from Aldair but that seemed like a deceitful thing to do to someone who'd been so cool with me.

I simply said, "I'm sorry. I'm not at liberty to say." I'm getting the hang of this "vague" thing. But at least it was the truth. What now? Torture? Mind meld? Bad attitude? No. Just a knowing look followed by a bland bowl of guacamole and chips. I was spoiled. Sam knew.

8

I'd been writing for about two hours while answering the occasional query from A or C. I liked them. They had an interesting manner. Sam let the whole guacamole thing go and Dave never mentioned it. Their conversation, their language was giving me a headache. When they reverted to telepathy, I could understand them. I gleaned that Abbott and Costello were reporters of some kind and were along for the ride.

Dave came over and sat down next to me. He gave me a small vial of liquid to drink saying this will make me feel better. Almost immediately it did. We had a nice conversation about the last few days, what my feelings on everything were and he apologized for the change of itinerary regarding the big first contact announcement of which, apparently, there would be none. He said that was not their decision but thought that ultimately it was the best decision. I had the feeling that it was something I did or didn't do, that I somehow wasn't up to snuff. He assured me that wasn't the case and it was, he hesitated, political. I told him about my philosophy of keeping snapshots or events in my memory, the old cell phone video thing, and he got it. I didn't remember if we went over this before, but I asked about the iPad. He said I could keep it for an earth day then it would return to the

Aldairans. I assumed I couldn't permanently erase anything that they couldn't retrieve and he asked why would I want to do that.

I said," Maybe I'm writing some things about you guys that I wouldn't want you to see." He looked a little taken aback and said, "Well, we'll see it. And how bad could it be?"

I said, "It's not." And I had a chance to really thank him and tell him what an amazing experience this had been. And that I hoped we could meet again but he said that wouldn't happen, "At least," he said, "not in this plane." Amazing just didn't say it. I'll have to invent a word.

I felt a real sense of closure and closeness with Dave at the moment and wondered, given their emotional status, how much, if any, of that he or Sam or anyone I'd met felt or could feel. Was this just an astronomical exercise or did a small sense of the possibility of a future earthly addition to the community rise up? I hoped they could see the possibility. We may need it.

9

We'd been heading, I assumed, back to earth for about forty-five minutes. Everyone was doing their own thing. There was a small area in the rear of the egg that had a comfortable looking captain's chair and nothing else. It'd be like sitting in the backward facing seat in the back of the old station wagons. Remember that? No seat belts. Just a lot of rolling around and awkward stares from the people behind you. Somehow, we survived. I went back and sat down and, of course, the seat molded to me perfectly and a small console popped up on the right side. It hung solidly in the air and I wasn't about to touch it. This felt like a private space and I needed some reflecting time.

The subject of competition stuck with me. A and C didn't get it and I saw no sign of it on Aldair. I never had a real competitive nature. I remember a cloud hanging over the bus ride back to Piscataway after the Piscataway High School football team's first loss. Guys were down. To be honest it didn't affect me that much. We played a good game, had fun, and lost. We also lost every game for the rest of the season. Ouch. I was at my most competitive during inter neighborhood play. From Knollwood we'd go up against Leo and the Boys. From Tara there was the Tarables. We were the Rivercrest Mob. Football was our strong suit, basketball was our Achilles heel and baseball could go either way. I wanted to win those games. Having to face Leo in study hall on the Monday following a game ignited my competitive spirit. And it was a rollicking good time. The winner's gloating would continue until the next go 'round.

I played in the Little League World Series, not the one in Williamsport. I played in the Plainfield, NJ Little League World Series. The year, 1962. I was on the Braves. Our side of town represented the National League and the other side represented the American League. We were pitted against the dreaded Indians. Plainfield had the minor league and major league and they were separated according to age and ability. My team, the Braves were in the minors and we were pumped. I wasn't sure why, as a lefty, I was playing shortstop but mine was not to reason why. I had been doing some pitching earlier in the year. When our coach was trying to figure out position placement earlier in the season, he had everyone take a crack at pitching. I was having one of those "in the zone" moments. I don't know where it came from, but I was throwing smokin' strikes that had a little jump on them. The coach was catching.

I started the home opener and proceeded to plunk the first two batters, pals of mine. So much for the "zone." I could still bring the heat but never knew where the ball was going to wind up. I settled in at first base, shortstop and had the occasional relief pitching stint. The season wore on and the Braves just kept on winning. As a team we were riding in the "zone."

And so, here we were, the Little League World Series. Our field on the corner of Rock and Myrtle Ave was pretty decked out as these fields went. We had dugouts, an outfield fence lined with advertisers and comfortable rows of bleachers on either side of the field. But the field on the other side of town, Seidler Field had LIGHTS....and...... infield grass.

Now here was the rub. Both managers were given the option to use players from the majors. Our manager went with what got us there. The other manager didn't. I always thought our manager made the right decision, even though the outcome was well sealed. Game one was at our field at Rock and Myrtle. I started at shortstop and batted second. We took the field and I settled into self-defense mode as the Indians started smacking rockets to short and third. I caught a few, missed a few and never saw a few. We didn't fare much better on offense. Bobby grounded out on the first pitch. I stepped in and it suddenly seemed like the distance between home and the pitcher's mound had noticeably shrunk. That was one big boy out there. Luckily, our coach gave me all the confidence I could possibly need with the old nugget, "C'mon Teddy. He puts his pants on one leg at a time, just like you." Really, again, that's what yer sending me out there with?

I never saw the first pitch, but the ump screamed, "Strike!" It sounded like a ball. Gargantua was throwing straight heat so I just dug in and swung cracking a line drive to second. The second baseman, sporting an elegant two-day growth of beard, reached up and put it away. We lost 22 – 0. Next stop was Seidler Field, under the lights. We went 1- 2 -3 in the top of the first but that was forgotten during the infield throw around under the lights to start the bottom of the first. I had one of those remember this feeling moments, as I did on the beach in Bermuda and on a mountain outside El Paso and next to a giant Redwood in northern California and doing somersaults in an empty black void waiting for a ride home.

The first Indian batter, all six feet of him, drilled a line drive right at me. It smacked into my glove and that was one away. And that was pretty much the highlight for me. Their pitcher was good but not as good as the other guy. They only beat us 18 – 2. I made some plays, blew some plays and had one hit. To my team's credit there was no bellyaching. We gave it our best shot and against all odds, lost. Some of the parents weren't happy with the situation. Mine were cool.

The Awards ceremony at Clinton school, my Kindergarten Alma Mater was a little awkward. We ate some rubber chicken and were handed our trophies. But standing on the stage next to the champion Indians the size and age difference was obvious. It was the elephant in the room. And then a strange thing happened. I went in thinking we were going to be embarrassed but somehow, we were standing tall and the Indians seemed a little "slouchy." Everyone in the room knew what was what. So, what is the life lesson? Once again, dance with the one what brung ya? Life's not fair? No crying in baseball? You decide. I hung onto my trophy for many years but somewhere along the line it disappeared. David vs Goliath. Everyone must deal with that at one time or another. As the song goes, "Sometimes you're the windshield, sometimes you're the bug." I've been both.

If you haven't guessed by now, I'm a dreamer. I've been known to miss two or three exits on the NJ Turnpike as I play my bass with the E Street Band or attempt to survive on a desert island or go traveling the cosmos with Sam and Dave. But this was no daydream. Abbott and Costello were standing on either side of me. Was I daydreaming that loud? I had a feeling they wanted to talk. I didn't. I'm still daydreaming. But I also had work to do. I'd been writing, trying to organize and there was a lot of information. Time would be short at home to get this all down and I was trying to make it as coherent as possible. No small task for a guy like me.

I wing a lot of things. On my first radio show twenty-eight years ago, I tried to be a grown up. I prepared the whole show and had everything in order; records, cds, cassettes, witticisms and a pithy story or two. As I stood at the top of the stairs in our second floor Locktown, NJ apartment at four thirty in the morning my cardboard cat carrier was stuffed. Apparently too stuffed as the cardboard handles ripped off and the cacophony of Stones, Beatles, Willie, plastic, vinyl and paper cascaded in slow motion down the eighteen or nineteen steps. Downstairs dogs were barking, and babies were crying as I scrambled to throw everything back in the box and make it to the WDVR studio in time for the National Anthem. I made it.

The show was chaotic, but it worked and that's the way I've done it ever since. That doesn't work for everyone, but it works for me. Sometimes I try to plan things, but it just doesn't jive. I'll see something interesting in New York or hear a comical story or a news headline that's begging for my unconventional slant. As mentioned earlier, I'll jot down a note but when it comes time to pull said note out during the show, I either can't read my own writing, or the context of the reference completely escapes me.

That loose style works for me, usually, on the radio, on the stage and in life. I once went to an open audition for Cats, the musical. I was working in the city and saw the open call announcement. It was in two hours and I was in the neighborhood. I didn't get a call back but a rockin' life experience was had. To quote the late, great George Gobel," Did you ever feel like you were a pair of brown shoes in a roomful of tuxedoes?" Yeah, like that.   Somehow, I've gotten this far treating life as the cosmic joke it obviously is. There are a few things in life I want to get right. This was one of them. I had everything fairly well organized and if I could get it all down at home before whatever was going to happen, happened, it'd be alright.

10

I was left alone to ponder the vastness of the universe and noticed stars. We were somewhere. Imagine this. I was in an alien spacecraft hurtling through creation with four aliens and yet I was enjoying being alone. A couple thoughts bear repeating, if only to remind myself. I was always comfortable being alone. As a kid I could amuse myself. As an adult I could amuse myself. Girlfriends were nice. Companionship was nice. I'd taken solo vacations and there's always a moment where you wish someone was next to you sharing this sunset, or hearing this band or sharing this conch soup. But alone was ok too.

Now I was thinking about home, about Linda and Molly and even Mickey, our feisty parakeet who loved to take small divots out of our lip or nose. What would I be walking into? How would I explain to a curious neighbor my stepping off an alien egg? Would the Aldairans decide to meet? How much would I remember and why would they allow or want my memory of this to fade? Where had I been?

There was something that had been on my mind. I've felt all along, right or wrong that Sam was the leader, the head of this expedition. I wanted to have a brief chat. I looked over at him and threw a telepathic "Yo!" at him. He looked up. I made it known that if he had a few minutes I'd like to ask a favor. He put up his finger in the "just a minute" gesture. It was that gangly pinky finger but I got the message. I went back to savoring the rapidly passing universe as the stars continued to get thicker, all the while opening and closing the iPad as thoughts, ideas and impressions rolled in. Was it my imagination or were the early stages of this escapade slowly slip sliding away?

A small jump seat opened next to me and Sam hopped in. He looked tired. I asked how he was feeling, and he said he had to recharge and that I should do the same. We had some hours of travel ahead of us including another darkness before we came to my star.

We were communicating without speaking. This was getting easier all the time and seemed so much more efficient. The only drawback for me was that because I didn't know their language a lot of thought transfer manifested in what I'd been calling impressions. The "darkness before your star" was, I think, an impression but it translated perfectly.

I told him I wanted to thank him for this uniquely singular experience, and I hoped I also brought something to the table for them. He had that deciphering look on his face and said, "Indeed you did." He and I were pondering the stars which were getting thinner, sparser. I said I appreciated, more than he could possibly know, the time and effort he'd taken to show me the wonders of the universe in this short time and humor me before I even knew I wanted to be humored. He said Aldairan thought communication takes a different path than thought. They can control and direct it. I was an open book. "Here and there, we took a shoot," he said.

I said, "Shot." Then I said, "You nailed it, my brother. Thank you so very much."

He looked at me curiously and said," So how did you get the guacamole on your face?" I looked back at him and with as mysterious a look as I could muster said, "What guacamole."

We went back to staring. I was telling him that the moon landing in 1969 was an event shared by our world. After staring up at the moon and wondering we could now look up and think that a chosen few of us had walked there. The moon has always held a certain mystery for us. It has been witness to proposals and marriages and is the unmoving romantic subject for painters and songwriters. It's one of the old reliables. You know when you look up and the nighttime skies allow, she will be there waiting for you, in all her phases. To me the moon is a lady; a lady who allows the man in the moon to rent some space, for now. She pushes and pulls our oceans and has allowed me many wonderful days of surfing and body surfing on NJ waves. The dinosaurs saw it. The early cave painters saw it. Socrates, Shakespeare, Washington, Lincoln and Elvis saw it. It's simply a part of us. I wasn't sure if I was saying this to me or Sam or just throwing it out there. Sam came as close to a chuckle as I'd seen so far.

"You want a close up look," he said.

"Yes," I declared emphatically. Why not. I had no idea what kind of schedule he was on, but I didn't think ten minutes would make a big difference. He didn't either. He suggested sleep as we would be leaving this system and crossing the void into Earth's system. He got up. I wrote for another twenty minutes, shrunk the pad and leaned back. The void.

11

I woke to an interstellar race. We were neck and neck with an asteroid the size of a small house. And Dave was on it. Ride 'em cowboy! He was holding something and moving it here and there, gathering readings of some kind. He chipped a small chunk and held it up. It vanished in his hand and materialized in a small clear container attached to the wall in the front of the egg.

The sense of non-movement as we were moving at these tremendous speeds was hard to digest. It was just one more item way beyond my comprehension. Dave pushed off and eased back into the egg. How fast were we traveling? I remember on our way out we crossed our solar system in ten minutes, or was it an hour? I guess I don't remember.

I was a big fan of Superman back in the day, comics and television show. After church on Sundays we'd stop at the local bakery for rolls and maybe a dessert of some kind. Gram would give me a dime and I'd bop into Prescott's next door for the latest Superman comic. When it went up to twelve cents, I really had to work her for the extra two cents. One of Superman's comic book adventures centered around displaying his powers by way of ten super feats for some reason. So, he did this and that, but his final super feat was flying across the solar system in ten seconds. He didn't quite make it because he stopped on Venus to rescue a Venusian cat stuck in a tree. We could still believe in the prospect of a Venusian society in the late fifties and early sixties. Superman failed. But he won because his greatest power was his super heart. Ain't that sweet?

Our crossing of the solar system. however quickly we crossed, wasn't Superman fast but certainly faster than we're going to see for quite a while barring an enlightenment, which is apparently on its way. I hope we recognize it.

I got up and moved to join the boys. A massive body was off to our right. As Dave was getting comfortable, he looked at me and said, "Welcome home." It was the sun. Our sun, like I've never seen it. I don't know how close we were but how close can you get to the sun without being profoundly affected? It was sputtering and throwing out plumes that seemed like they might hit us. Everything was moving on the surface. It was alive. Without it, of course, our planetary system was nothing, another cold void with nine huge empty rocks and a few moons. One day it will burn itself out having provided nothing less than life, generation upon generation of life. By then I guess we'd better be ready to move.

We pulled away and really picked it up just as we hit turbulence. It was a strange, gliding kind of turbulence, the kind of soft rolling you get at some point during a roller coaster ride. That went on for about thirty seconds and the gang seemed to be enjoying the ride. I thought maybe we were riding a solar flare or some effect of our sun. I'll have to remember this the next time I'm body surfing down the Jersey shore.

Abbott and Costello were working wall screens as Sam and Dave looked to be concentrating on keeping the egg on course. I asked if I could have some water and Abbott ordered me one up. I'd had a great rest and felt like I was as ready as I could be for whatever was coming next. I got to work on the iPad one last time. When I looked up again, I felt like we weren't moving. I'd been facing to the rear which was a relative position in space but when I looked around, there she was. Mother Earth was rising up behind a glorious, brilliant moon. I was, indeed home. Almost.

12

True to his word Sam brought us up and over the surface of our moon, past earthly debris and a beautiful red, white and blue flag. He continued until I realized he was waiting for me to say stop. We pulled up and over a small mountain range and glided along a smooth stretch when I said," stop." Everyone suited up. I just had to pull on my helmet and gloves. I felt like I was back on a NJ beach with my pals as we climbed into our wetsuits and prepared for the plunge into the surf. Dave gave me an adjustment and I was goin' moonwalking.

I slipped out first and was primed for the bouncing moon walk we'd been accustomed to seeing. I stepped out onto the surface of the moon and just started walking. I inquired. Sam came over and made an adjustment. I started doing the moon bounce. Now this was the experience. After a few minutes I asked to be tweaked back to the flat-footed incarnation. Sam tweaked and I was again walking. Dave remained in the egg and Abbott and Costello were taking pictures or videos of some kind. They seemed to be focusing on me a lot. I found a comfortable looking rock and sat. I was picking up dust and letting it slip through my fingers. Moon dust.

The earth was more stunning than in any picture or video I've ever seen. Like the beaches in Bermuda you just had to be there. And like the folks who have seen the Earth from this perspective one of the first things that jumps out at you is the lack of earthly borders. They're man made. That's an obvious observation but that is what I thought. The other thing is seeing the thin atmosphere that tenuously clings to our Mother. How does it not blow away? Everything is in such perfect balance. And to think of all the things that had to work together, had to go just right to get us here; the right amount of carbon, oxygen, carbon dioxide, element after element, water and on and on. It all worked. Of all the places I've just seen this blue marble takes the blue ribbon. I got up and walked. It was like walking on a beach with the Earth watching over me. This was it. No soundtrack needed.

I was about two hundred yards away when I heard, "Time to go." I climbed a small rise and looked all around. Three hundred and sixty degrees. I continued toward the ship and saw a nice even patch of sandy ground. I bent over and wrote, "Lyons, 2018. I came in peace." Too heavy? It may blow someone's mind someday and prove my case if it comes to that. I was the last one on board. Sam took a quick head count and we were off again. There was no kick up of moon dust. I suggested a fly-by of the International space station. They exchanged semi amused glances. This would be cool. I was standing up in front of the egg almost on top of the windshield. After a minute I saw it. We trailed it for about ten seconds then sped by, not too fast. I want to hear the explanation for that. I never did.

I asked once again if this was it. There'd be no White House lawn landing, no spectacular fly by, no take me to your leader? I was told, in no uncertain terms, not this time. It was not their decision to make but they had thought up until recently that this was to be the time. It wasn't. I asked if they would at least come in for a cup of coffee. An uncomfortable head shake. Well, waddaya know, they seemed embarrassed. I didn't want to leave it like this. I thanked everyone again and said I understood but I'm telling anyone who will listen anyway. Sam said that was fine but do it soon. "You won't remember." he solemnly said.

We'd been moving and Mother Earth was coming up fast. Then we were entering Earth's atmosphere. I asked if they needed my address and almost got a chuckle. The lights dimmed and I recognized the Delaware River. We came in low, hung a sweeping right past the red barn, (I hear ya, Gram) up and over the trees and down into my back yard.

"Well, this is where I came in," I said. Sam and Dave each gave me a bro hug. Abbott and Costello opted for the weird Aldairan elbow grab. What was that, anyway? I was wearing the suit and had the iPad.

Dave said," We mentioned this before but the iPad as you call it, and as we will from now on, will return in a day and a half. The suit in an hour. We have to have them back." Sam handed me my clothes. They looked strange. I stepped out and Sam stepped out behind me. "Peace," he said and flashed the universal sign. "And where did you get that guacamole on your mustache?"

"Lucas," I said. Flashing back the sign I said, "Peace, my brother. Safe travels." I had that walking down the runway at the airport feeling. You know it. The sad goodbye, then the final turn around followed by the deep exhale; the letting go of whatever's being let go, temporarily or permanently, followed by a sense of excitement and a touch of fear and uncertainty, but mostly excitement.

I was still in sad goodbye mode when I heard or more like felt, the departure of my friends and the end of the cosmic adventure of a lifetime. Something was slipping away. I felt a sense of urgency. I'd been staring over my house, at the moon. I knew it well. I came in peace. I quickly looked back and up. There was nothing there. There was everything there. I heard a door and a soft, frightened, "Ted." I turned and exhaled one more time. "Oh honey, I'm home. "

The End

**

Epilogue

**

I was gone for three days. I thought Sam had said four. Looking at the number of notes I've compiled I don't see how that's possible. Space times time equals I don't know what. Maybe it was three days. Given the ground covered the speed of light must have been greatly exceeded. Add the solar winds and the weird wormhole like paths and I guess anything is possible. The cool wetsuit and the iPad went home when I wasn't looking, as promised. As of now the preceding events seem like a blurry memory, like a story you've heard so many times you feel like you were actually there. Throughout the scribblings are the warnings of memory loss, and the distinct probability of no backup from the Aldairans. Even my handwritten notes, scribblings are becoming hard to locate or seem to be wandering off. For some reason, this compilation has been allowed to stay. I think they want us to know, to have an optimistic hope.

Linda discreetly covered for me. She was about to confide in our neighbor when I turned up. I disappeared through the weekend and a little beyond.

We've both gotten very foggy on the whole thing, more each day. When I think about it or we try to talk about it a slight feeling of nausea washes over me, a quite different kind of nausea. Not that unpleasant but enough to bring me back to the here and now. I also have this invigorated, hopeful, faith in the future of humanity presence that I'm carrying around. I'm not sure why but I know everything will be all right.

I let some time go by before really digging into writing about my "Lost Weekend." I thought it might bring back a more distinct memory. It hasn't. All the close encounter experiences I've ever read about involved total memory loss recovered only through hypnosis. I've considered going that route but not now. I filled Linda in on the whole thing the night I came back but it's fading out on her too. Going back and scanning parts of my story, it reads like a piece of fiction. But parts jump out in a flash of brilliant memory. I can see it, smell it. Then, it's gone. Except for Lucas. He feels real. I feel him around me from time to time. A guardian angel?

I still stand out in my back yard at night and throw out the same "prayer" to the universe that I always have. "If you're there, come down." No answer. But at least now I know.... they're there.

**

CPSIA information can be obtained
at www.ICGtesting.com
Printed in the USA
LVHW030824201120
672005LV00005B/216